PENGUIN BOOKS

THE LITTLE PRINCE
AND LETTER TO A HOSTAGE

Antoine de Saint-Exupéry was born into an old French family in 1900. Despite his father's death in 1904 he had an idyllic childhood, shared with his brother and three sisters at the family's château near Lyon. He was educated at a strict Jesuit school in Le Mans and then at the college of Saint-Jean in Fribourg. Against the wishes of his family he qualified as a pilot during his national service, and flew in France and North Africa until his demobilization in 1923. Unsuited to civilian life and deeply hurt by a failed relationship with the writer Louise de Vilmorin, he returned to his first love, flying. In 1926 he joined the airline Latécoère, later to become Aéropostale, as one of its pioneering aviators, charged with opening mail routes to remote African colonies and to South America with primitive planes and in dangerous conditions. As airfield manager at the tiny outpost of Cape Juby in Morocco his duties included rescuing stranded pilots from rebel tribesmen, and it was there that he wrote *Southern Mail*, which was well received on its publication in 1929. From a later posting to Buenos Aires he bought the manuscript of *Night Flight* back to France, together with his fiancée, the beautiful but tempremental Consuelo Suncin. *Night Flight* was awarded the Prix Femina in 1931, firmly establishing his literary reputation. Flying and writing were inseparable elements in his passionate creativity, but he was not a model pilot; he was nonchalant about checks, and tended to lapse into reveries at the controls. His career was chequered with near-fatal crashes and on 30 January 1935 he came down in the Libyan desert while attempting to break the Paris–Saigon record. The story of his miraculous survival is told in *Wind, Sand and Stars*. At the outbreak of the Second World War he was too old to fly a fighter but flew in a reconnaissance squadron until the French surrender in t   he wrote
the essay *Letter to a Ho*   hildren's
fable for which he is   vritten of
his war experiences   bestseller

D1512049

list for six months in 1942, and was banned by the Vichy government in France. However, he refused to support de Gaulle and as a result was vilified by the General's Free French supporters. Depressed by this and his troubled marriage, he persuaded Allied commanders in the Mediterranean to let him fly again, and it was in July 1944 that he disappeared, almost certainly shot down over the sea by a German fighter.

T. V. F. Cuffe was educated in Dublin and at the Sorbonne. He has also translated Voltaire's *Micromégas* and is completing a new translation of *Candide* for Penguin Classics.

THE LITTLE PRINCE

AND

LETTER TO A HOSTAGE

Antoine de Saint-Exupéry

Translated by

T. V. F. CUFFE

PENGUIN BOOKS

PENGUIN BOOKS

Published by the Penguin Group
Penguin Books Ltd, 80 Strand, London WC2R ORL, England
Penguin Putnam Inc., 375 Hudson Street, New York, New York 10014, USA
Penguin Books Australia Ltd, Ringwood, Victoria, Australia
Penguin Books Canada Ltd, 10 Alcorn Avenue, Toronto, Ontario, Canada M4V 3B2
Penguin Books India (P) Ltd, 11 Community Centre, Panchsheel Park, New Delhi – 110 017, India
Penguin Books (NZ) Ltd, Cnr Rosedale and Airborne Roads, Albany, Auckland, New Zealand
Penguin Books (South Africa) (Pty) Ltd, 24 Sturdee Avenue, Rosebank 2196, South Africa

Penguin Books Ltd, Registered Offices: 80 Strand, London WC2R ORL, England

www.penguin.com

The Little Prince first published as *Le Petit Prince* and simultaneously
in English translation by Reynal & Hitchcock 1943
Letter to a Hostage first published as *Lettre à un otage* by Brentano's 1943
First English translation (*Southern Mail*) translated by Stuart Gilbert,
These translations first published in Penguin Books 1995
Vol de Nuit first published by Gallimard 1931
Reprinted with colour illustrations 1998
Reprinted in Penguin Classics 2000
17 16

Set in Monotype Baskerville
Typeset by Datix International Limited, Bungay, Suffolk
Printed in China by South China Printing Company

978-0-14-118562-0

CONTENTS

INTRODUCTION

This volume brings together two works written during
Antoine de Saint-Exupéry's wartime exile in the United
States and published in New York in the spring of 1943.
The Little Prince and the *Letter to a Hostage* make strange
bedfellows: a children's story and an open letter to a
Jewish intellectual in hiding in occupied France. They are
juxtaposed in time, but to bring them together in one
place is to suggest other affinities, and this may seem an
unlikely way of presenting *The Little Prince* – a story which
has been delighted in for its timeless charm and trans-
parency, whose appeal so transcends age and nationality as
to have made it the most translated book in the French
language.

But there is something to be said for situating such a
work. Just as children's classics are always considered to
speak for everyone (for adults, for children – regardless of
the divisions within and even between these groups), so too
they are read as somehow occasionless: independent of the
pressures and circumstances which produce them just as
they produce any literary work. In the case of *The Little
Prince*, these circumstances were urgent and inauspicious,
and this charming story was conceived *in extremis*, at the
crisis point of an entire life.

The conundrum – the scandal, almost – of this story is
that it was written in exile, in time of war, by a childless
man of action agonized by his enforced inactivity, by the

fate of his country and by the nature of a post-war world. Readers familiar with Saint-Exupéry's life and death have felt that *The Little Prince*, ostensibly for children, is perhaps a piece of autobiography – an attempt to sublimate the difficulties of his marriage, or to fend off the present for a remembered world of childhood, or even an act of mysterious farewell. It may be all of these things, but *The Little Prince* also addresses its broader occasions in the pared-down terms of a parable for children. What this book might mean for adults, including its author, is the subject of this introduction.

By December 1940, when he sailed for New York, Saint-Exupéry was forty years old and a celebrated writer-aviator. Born into a large and well-connected Catholic aristocratic family, he spent his childhood within a matriarchal household, in the setting of a large chateau near Lyon, an immense garden and a nearby airfield. Saint-Exupéry claimed in adult life to have been delivered early and irreparably into unhappiness, sent to school in the rigid conservative and royalist establishments of his class and time, where he fared poorly. He finished school as the First World War ended, but passed out of military service in 1923 with a pilot's licence.

· He was to spend much of his life as a young man in the air, intensively so between 1926 and 1932, when he flew for what was later to become the Aéropostale, the Latécoère company – first carrying the mail from Toulouse to Morocco, then taking charge of a remote and ill-equipped airstrip at Cape Juby (a West African desert outpost bordering the Atlantic). Thereafter he moved to Buenos Aires, where he helped pioneer a network of aerodromes along the coast of Patagonia, opening up South America to a regular mail-carrying service.

Saint-Exupéry's formative years of flight coincided with the great age of French aviation inaugurated by Blériot, when flying was seen as both patriotic engagement and heroic individualism, camaraderie and solitary self-reliance. Saint-Exupéry was admired by contemporaries like André Gide for leading an exemplary life in which action and writing, freedom and duty were fused; Sartre was later to describe Saint-Exupéry as the precursor of a literature of the machine (*littérature de l'outil*), of construction rather than consumption.

In his early books, *Southern Mail* (*Courrier sud*, 1928) and *Night Flight* (*Vol de nuit*, 1931), Saint-Exupéry devised a modern mythology of aviation. Flying obsessed him above everything else because it allowed him to think *about* everything else – namely the fundamental questions which the heroic age of flight posed anew in such existentially available form. And Saint-Exupéry's peripatetic cast of mind tended from the outset towards an inclusive view of experience.

Nietzsche's aphorism, 'If one has character one also has one's typical experience which recurs again and again', seems peculiarly suited to Saint-Exupéry. But between 1932 and the outbreak of the Second World War the digressive focus of his experiment in living had become increasingly difficult to maintain. His flying career was jeopardized both by the financial crises of the Latécoère company and by his own tendency to crash his planes – notably in the Libyan desert in 1935, where he spent three days aimlessly wandering and nearly died of thirst before being rescued. His marriage in 1931 to Consuelo Suncin, a vivacious and single-minded Salvadorean whom he had met in Buenos Aires, was itself an affair of famously self-consuming intricacy and uncertainty.

If Saint-Exupéry's vocation steadily unravelled, the individual voice and the shapes of his writing were consolidated in these years. Beginning in erratic and verbose bouts of journalism, his method was drastically to refine upon these premature growths until he had achieved an elliptical brevity. The process was perfected in *Wind, Sand and Stars (Terre des hommes)* – an exhaustively rewritten collection of articles and essays on flying, the men who flew, the desert, and Saint-Exupéry's experiences as a correspondent during the Spanish Civil War – whose publication in 1939 made him famous on both sides of the Atlantic.

When war broke out, despite his age and adverse medical reports, he secured a posting to a high-level reconnaissance unit based in the Marne. After a few experimental flights in the new fast planes with which the unit was equipped, Saint-Exupéry was sent out in May 1940 with a fighter escort to overfly the town of Arras, after the German offensive was well under way. This disastrous mission (the town was already ablaze, Saint-Exupéry's unit ran into a wall of anti-aircraft fire, two of his escort were shot down by Messerschmidts) was recounted in *Flight to Arras (Pilote de guerre)* published in 1942. Shortly afterwards the remnants of this unit joined the general retreat, moving southwards by stages to North Africa, and with the armistice in operation he was now demobilized.

Between the armistice and his departure for America, Saint-Exupéry tried to discover an appropriate course of action. Believing that France was by now too weak to confront the Germans without results from which she would never recover, he chose not to respond to the general call to resistance issued by de Gaulle from London. He instinctively distrusted de Gaulle's politics, and feared that his initiatives would lead to an outbreak of civil war in France such as he had witnessed as a journalist in Spain. However, although he held a low opinion of the Vichy administration, he was conservatively sympathetic to Pétain's call for a return to traditional values. For Saint-Exupéry as for many of his class, Vichy represented legitimacy and continuity – a contrast to the discredited Republic which had failed to prepare France for war, but also its recognizable heir.

By going to New York Saint-Exupéry had decided to campaign from abroad through his writing, and to act on his settled conviction that the United States must be stirred from neutrality. But exile was also an admission of his failure to find a way forward amid conflicting choices as an actor in the tragedy of his country. The peacetime heroes of his books had been figures of single-minded and unqualified loyalties, and Saint-Exupéry's life as a commercial aviator had been 'a sort of war', since the ethos of the Aéropostale was to transfer the idea of man's expendability from the field of battle to the delivery of mail.

These, then, are the bare elements of Saint-Exupéry's predicament from December 1940 to April 1943, during which he conceived and wrote *The Little Prince*. The story is a *jeu d'esprit*, but it has its roots in despair. What Saint-Exupéry had to say could be articulated most economically in the Morse code of a children's story, by a putting of the complex into the simple. And in many stylistic respects *The Little Prince* is a logical development from *Wind, Sand and Stars*.

THE PRINCE

The narrative of the little boy who lived on a planet scarcely bigger than himself, who wanders about the universe and lands on Earth, where he meets an aviator who has crashed in the desert, might seem a fragile receptacle for the burdens I have outlined. But part of the story's appeal has always been its refusal to accept that version of childhood which confuses the fragility of the child's situation with an incapacity for moral understanding. For Saint-Exupéry, as for Henry James, children can bear a great deal of reality; the child is a conscience as well as a consciousness. By the same token, childhood – as Freud had confirmed – can no longer innocently be described as a state of innocence.

In every age run-of-the-mill children's literature has supported the status quo (part of whose baggage is the cult of childhood innocence), just as good children's literature has subverted it by stressing the recalcitrance of childhood to our correct notions of civic, collective virtue. Children are not miniature adults, as the Lockean account would have it; nor even is the child the father to the man, as Romanticism suggests, since that, too, proposes a unity in our lives which is over-economical with the two truths of childhood and adulthood. The enfranchised image of childhood as a state of difference – neither straightforwardly lapsarian nor prelapsarian – might be said to begin with Victorian nonsense, that astonishing invention of a looking-glass society with its own protocols, its free-floating anxiety and precarious fantasy, its own language, truth and logic.

The Little Prince is at least partly in this tradition. Not only is the hero an alien (an alien because a child), he is in effect the only non-human person in the humanized solar system of the story. Not strictly a child at all, he is certainly very *like* a little boy. But even his gender is uncertain. Moreover the grown-up world is at least as odd as the child's. Both are dream states, and no confrontation is stranger than the child's with the man. Like Lewis Carroll's Alice, Saint-Exupéry's prince moves through a world of mystifying adult behaviour. Both stories describe a learning process (as they must: childhood is another country but also a waiting-room, a state of accommodation and accept-ance), where hero or heroine try to make sense of the rules by which adults live.

Saint-Exupéry's story describes the education of a prince – an old humanist topic – but a Rousseauesque education which is designed to protect the child in him from social institutions and their insidious palsy. The learning process is partly achieved before the prince reaches the Earth, during his Grand Tour of the other six planets. His brief galactic encounters allude to a tradition in French literature of Utopian speculation on the existence of other worlds, going back, via Voltaire's *Micromégas*, to Cyrano de Bergerac. (When the little prince falls to Earth, in a norma-tive gesture taken directly from this tradition, he at first thinks it uninhabited.) To the fantastic voyage or quest is added the device of the alien visitor, rather as Montesquieu employed this in his *Lettres persanes*. One of Saint-Exupéry's unpublished drawings beautifully blends these elements – showing the little prince dressed in top hat and tails, speculatively floating above an empty planet containing a single house, its chimney smoking.[1]

If there is life elsewhere, such works ask, how is it

governed? Is there an ideal state? The little prince learns how to run his own small but unpredictable planet, with its rose, its baobabs (the baobab is the African tree of life, which in this story is a tree of death), its volcanoes, its mysterious tendency to anarchy. Or rather what he learns is how not to govern. The six characters whom he meets (the king, the conceited man, the drinker, the businessman, the lamplighter, the geographer) all turn out to be disordered personalities – not cruel or mad as are the adults in *Alice in Wonderland*, but certainly rude, foolish and arbitrary. Each is alone on his planet, his solipsistic bubble-world, and the anamorphic distortion of some of the drawings suggests the autistic remoteness of these figures.

These hermetically sealed adults are not only solitary but also needy and demanding, since company is what adults – unlike children – most inordinately desire. This hapless combination provides the formal comedy of the prince's brief encounters, and gives them their Alice-like energies. The exchanges between child and adult are peremptory and astringent, with a dream-like lack of preamble, in which characters accost each other with truths, contradictions, questions ('That's a funny hat you're wearing'). Conversation is a terrain to be fought over, a power struggle but also an open sesame: asking the right questions produces instructive answers, clues as to what comes next.

But here the affinities with Alice could be said to end. *The Little Prince* has things to say about language in a moral sense (as a source of human misunderstanding, a quandary), but not in an extra-moral sense. It investigates value rather than meaning. The verbal play of the Alice books is quite foreign to the laconic stoicism of Saint-Exupéry's story. What the former explore, what Freud was to explore, is a difficulty in language: in speaking to others – and above all when we speak to children – we are in danger of speaking against ourselves. Two investigations are in play here, or rather one relationship, that between our insecure tenure within language and our insecure tenure in the fixtures and fittings of adult life. And because *The Little Prince* chooses not to engage this debate about meaning what we say, his story could be said to have no unconscious.

Put differently, whereas the Alice books are about the private category of nonsense, *The Little Prince* is about the political category of the absurd. Saint-Exupéry's writings have often been charged with conservatism; in technique as in politics, their face is turned away from the discoveries of modernism. But in *The Little Prince* Saint-Exupéry could equally be said to have grafted the generic discoveries of the children's story since Carroll (its logical atomism, its lack of a priori designs upon its readers) on to an absurdist image of the human condition as this was being formulated by contemporary European philosophy.

Thus the planets which the little prince visits are miniature theatres of the absurd, whose anachronistic inhabitants condemn themselves or are condemned to repeat an unbroken series of pointless acts. The conceited man wears a hat for saluting people, but no one ever passes his way. The king has no subjects, only a rat whom he must alternately condemn and pardon, so as to exercise (in both instances) his authority. The businessman counts stars which he can only nominally lay claim to owning; the geographer counts mountains and rivers he has never seen. And the lamplighter follows disembodied orders of sinister absurdity, lighting up and extinguishing as his planet turns more and more rapidly on its axis.[2] (*The Little Prince* was published in the same year as Albert Camus's *The Myth of Sisyphus*.)

The lamplighter is an especially charged example, since his absurd occupation is deeply sympathetic to the prince, a master who identifies with service and servant figures (as children do) and who refuses any of the images of kingship or ownership or mastery which are offered to him on his travels. But the lamplighter also epitomizes the unintelligibility of adult action. As a child in an adult world the little prince is an alien, and the adult world he observes is itself both alien and alienated from itself. But whereas a story like *Alice in Wonderland* emphasizes the unaccountability and hidden motivation of adults, in *The Little Prince* the emphasis is upon the child's accommodation to sheer motivelessness, the extreme case of which is war.[3]

If all children's fiction is about the impossible relation between adult and child, *The Little Prince* is unusual in addressing this theme directly. The generational gap which the story so strikingly insists upon (children must be tolerant towards grown-ups; grown-ups understand nothing about children) is a projection of war and its incomprehensibility on to the screen of child–adult conflict. By the time the prince arrives on Earth his reservations about grown-ups are in place; they merely need testing against a broader range of examples, on the planet which is, so to speak, the home of adulthood. Indeed, the various preliminary planets are an exploded diagram of our human world turned upside-down and fragmented into competing solipsisms. The social contract has broken down. Peacetime activities and transactions – taking trains, counting money, keeping time – have themselves become suspect: at once collective but meaningless; or meaningless because collective (war as such being the ultimate group activity).[4]

The little prince refuses any suggestion that in life the many outweigh the one. Grown-ups are shown as helplessly in thrall to numbers and to an idea of value as multiplication. Thus the businessman counting stars, the garden full of roses, the packed trains – even the self-multiplying echo on the mountain – are all negative images of plenitude, of inflation. The prince comes from a planet where there is only one of everything (like Crusoe's island in Elizabeth Bishop's poem 'Crusoe in England'), and he clings to an intuitive vision of value – one sheep, one rose, one well – as inhering in a Romantic symbolism of singularity and uniqueness.

Part of the drollery of the story is to confront him with ironic versions of such singularity: the rat, the May bug, the lowly desert flower by the wayside. For he clearly has a lesson to learn in this respect. Had life on his planet been so perfect he would not have needed to seek out other examples of a social contract at work. It is the fox who will teach him how to discriminate, how to discover value and singularity within the multitude, even if it is the fox himself who is most unforgiving about the way we live now – when everything is bought ready-made in shops – as a form of oblivion. But isolationism is no answer, as the airman (the other conscience in the story) knows to his cost.

THE AIRMAN

Like everyone else in his story, the narrator is alone, marooned in the solitude of the desert, and in the desert of his solitude. He is a somewhat old-fashioned and moralizing presence, but this is countered both by his heterodox view of childhood and by his portrayal of himself as a misfit, a passive revenant trapped between the worlds of the grown-up and the child.

By the same token he is a go-between, which he defends as the only position (fractured though it be) from which a story for children is at all tellable. Unlike the amnesiac grown-ups alluded to in the dedication of *The Little Prince*, who mislay their memory of ever having been children, the airman sees childhood as both a continuing story that persists into adulthood, and as the place of origins, where an older form of culture is preserved. His isolation and conservatism lie in his being able so acutely to recall a time before the present (a time when, for example, there were lamplighters instead of electricity).

Children's stories are about growing up and about refusing to grow up. Like Carroll, Saint-Exupéry wanted to have the advantages of being at once childish and adult, and in many respects his life was a Janus-like affair, pointing forward and backward. Even as a technician in the early days of mass communication, a man who epitomized modernity, he was anomalous. The open-cockpit and primitively equipped planes in which Saint-Exupéry spent his Aéropostale years were themselves a brief interlude in the history of aviation. A new thing in an old world, they rapidly became an old thing in a new world, and Saint-Exupéry was caught at this crossroads, both a pioneer and a belated figure.

This engineer-aristocrat was also politically divided. For most of his life he tried to reconcile a seigneurial traditionalism with a quasi-mystical belief in brotherhood and classless comradeship. The emphasis of his earlier books upon duty as the blind acceptance of orders was subsequently modified and is exorcized in the lamplighter chapter of *The Little*

Prince. The timid and obedient lamplighter ('orders are orders') is not only cannon-fodder, he is also a citizen of the future state. Half-enthralled though Saint-Exupéry was by the new American order of things, he sensed that democracy held in store forms of regimentation more subtle than but just as fearful as fascism, controlling people's needs by a somatic materialist appeal to their desires. Saint-Exupéry's unfinished and posthumously published prose epic, *Citadel* (*Citadelle*, 1948), transcribes the enigmatic parables of a Berber chieftain in his desert stronghold, advocating a static and traditionalist social order dispensed by a benign hereditary ruler.

The idiosyncratic humanism of *The Little Prince* is spelled out in the conversations between the fox and the little prince. The fox is on the side of a return to anachronistic social forms mediated by rituals, since modern estrangement shows itself precisely in the elimination of distance between people. Rituals, on the other hand, constitute a formality between friends and an intimacy between strangers. They are therefore ambivalent in ways suggestive of Saint-Exupéry's own psychology: a passionate philosopher of friendship, he was also in practice extremely reserved, his need of social barriers equalled by his vision of barriers circumvented (rather than broken). Rituals circulate a social energy, a tact which enables the privileged to share crucial experiences with the less privileged, bypassing the petrified conventions of the bourgeoisie. For Saint-Exupéry, a ritual is the antithesis of a convention.

Above all, rituals bypass language, which in *The Little Prince* is represented as the source of all misunderstanding, even as a form of shamelessness. (Saint-Exupéry was loquacious and loved conversation; he would also have agreed with Cardinal Newman's dictum that conversation is sinful.) Language, after all, is part of the visible order, which is consistently undermined by the moral essentialism of *The Little Prince*. The concealed (the unspoken, the complicit) are shown to be richly alive in the imaginative world of the story: whether the elephant inside the boa constrictor, the sheep inside its box, the seeds in the earth, the fox in his hole, the secret well in the Sahara, or the treasure buried in the old house. When the fox teaches the prince the forgotten ritual of taming – of 'creating ties' – he is making possible a relationship which obviates the need for words, like the silent smile in *Letter to a Hostage* which unites Saint-Exupéry with the bargemen or with the anarchist militiamen.

LETTER TO A HOSTAGE

Published in New York in February 1943, two months before *The Little Prince*, this text is an adult commentary upon the children's story that was to follow, though Saint-Exupéry was not presenting in either work a doctrinaire belief system so much as repeating and working through an obsessional knot of images. Saint-Exupéry's habits of mind were cerebral but also roundabout and compulsive.

These texts also share a consolatory occasion: the *Letter to a Hostage* addressed to and *The Little Prince* dedicated to Saint-Exupéry's close friend, the French Jewish intellectual and pacifist Léon Werth. From 1940 onwards French Jews – in the occupied zone but equally under Vichy rule – had been subject to increasingly comprehensive anti-Semitic statutes which prepared the way for mass deportation. Léon Werth spent the war in hiding in the Jura, and Saint-Exupéry would have received no news of him after arriving in the United States. He could only assume that his friend was still alive. The *Letter* is a private epistle, but also a digest of longstanding preoccupations and a public contribution, written in the spirit of the 'Open Letter to Frenchmen Everywhere' which Saint-Exupéry had published in *The New York Times* in November 1942 (when France became totally occupied).

From the solitude of one exile the *Letter* addresses another, since France has become a place of exile to its own inhabitants, doubly so as far as its Jewish population is concerned. The predicament of exile is generally implicit in the little prince's planetary wanderings, and the image of France in the *Letter* as a ship adrift in the night has its counterpart in the stranded narrator of the children's story, more isolated than a castaway on a raft in mid-ocean. Both texts share a rhetoric of light as community and of darkness as isolation, and the various geography lessons imparted by *The Little Prince* are a kind of wish-fulfilment: the sun setting over France while it is still noon in America brings in train the fantasy of getting to France in a twinkling, of keeping the lines of communication open; the memory of the army of lamplighters across the Earth in the days before electricity elegizes the dance of human settlement and continuity across the planet.

In opposition to this, the *Letter* conjures up for its American readership the darkened cities of wartime Europe ('the colour of cinders in a grate', when viewed from the air) and the false lights of wartime Lisbon, whose brazenly lit neutrality is as sterile as it is seductive. When Saint-Exupéry decided in December 1940 to flee to New York he was not permitted to cross fascist Spain, because he had reported on the Spanish Civil War from the Republican side. He therefore took ship from North Africa to Lisbon, sailing onwards to New York with a group of French refugees. His account of the motley expatriates bound for the New World is one of the most eloquent set-pieces in the psychology of modern exile. Its distinction between exile and expatriation, as respectively true and false states of being, repeats the battle-lines of *The Little Prince*. The rootless émigrés huddled around the roulette tables in Lisbon, like shades in the underworld, call to mind all the unnecessary roses and foxes, all the displaced and untamed beings who people the margins of the children's story. And the ghost ship of exiles in the *Letter*, whose future is their past, is opposed to that other very real ship – France, drifting in the night – whose precious human cargo holds in its communal past the real future, silenced but intact.

The only individuals on board who seemed real to Saint-Exupéry – he describes how he wanted to touch them for reassurance – were the crew, those men and women who silently carried dishes, polished brass, bore messages; who, in the stratified society of the time, were themselves habitually regarded as ghosts. One of the main themes of *The Little Prince* and the *Letter* is the secret link between friendship and what might seem to be its negation: the idea of service. Later on in the *Letter* Saint-Exupéry refers to the 'sacerdotal maidservant' who waited upon himself and Werth at a French riverside inn on a sunny pre-war afternoon. He recalls how the two friends invited a couple of bargemen to share the strange euphoria of the moment which had overtaken them. This gesture of unmediated friendship across a social divide was itself crucially mediated by the ceremony of serving and being served.

In *The Little Prince* the same complex of ideas is present – in the image of the prince serving his flower, or of the fox being tamed, or in the story's identification with public servants like the Turkish astronomer or the lamplighter or the railway pointsman. Friendship is an act of reaching across, and friends are those we befriend: the call made by like to unlike (the adult to the child, the fox to the boy, Werth and Saint-Exupéry to the bargees, the journalist to his anarchist captors). And it is this that Saint-Exupéry the patrician gentile describes himself as prizing most in his friendship with Werth the Trotskyist Jew: their unlikeness, their solidarity in difference. Just as the *Letter* insists that it is for the very survival of difference that a world war is being waged.

The Little Prince is a story of meetings and chance encounters, and Saint-Exupéry was imbued with the ancient belief that the stranger, the person you meet casually, might be a god in disguise. This connects with his absurdist humanism, and its insistence that we are bound each to each by natural piety. We are in a manner of speaking each other's gods, since we have no access to transcendence, to a god as such. In the face of the incomprehensible we can communicate only with each other, even if communicable experience ('the land of tears' in *The Little Prince*) is all but impossible. There is perhaps in the world of that story the added and hovering sense that grown-ups have no need of God as judge: the judgement of children is remorseless enough.

'A GARDEN WALL AT HOME MAY ENCLOSE MORE SECRETS THAN THE GREAT WALL OF CHINA'

For all that Saint-Exupéry's thought is didactic and portentous in style, it is also anti-dogmatic, proffering an experiential and tentative lay morality akin to that of Camus. In its procedures it is antithetical, as though moral questions presented themselves to Saint-Exupéry exclusively in the form of paradoxes.

This dialectic is engaged whenever he discusses the desert. (Saint-Exupéry belongs to that European cultural moment which embraced 'the religion of the sands' – an orientalism which he shares with contemporary kindred spirits and emissaries like Isabelle Eberhart or Pierre Loti.) In the *Letter*, as in *The Little Prince* and elsewhere, the Sahara is the privileged site of memory and individuality, and of Saint-Exupéry's strongest intuitions into the relation between the individual and the community. Where is the real desert? – 'not where one thinks it is. The Sahara is more alive than a metropolis, and the most teeming city is emptied of life if the essential poles of existence are demagnetized' (p. 104).

What polarizes the desert above all is Saint-Exupéry's domestic imagination, his visionary homelessness. In the *Letter* the Sahara is traversed by the memory of a childhood home; that is what constitutes its 'secret musculature'. In *Wind, Sand and Stars*, awaiting rescue after one of his innumerable crash landings, Saint-Exupéry falls into oneiric repossession of his childhood ('I saw once more the great solemn cupboards of the house, half open to show piles of sheets as white as snow').[5] Similarly in *Flight to Arras*, returning from his deadly sortie over the blazing city of

Arras – and characteristically pleased with himself for having lingered long enough to stare death in the face – Saint-Exupéry thinks of himself as 'a housewife taking the homeward road after finishing her shopping'.[6] *The Little Prince*, whose desert conceals a well as an old house hides buried treasure, abounds in cherished and paradoxical images of indwelling – not least the invention of a planet no bigger than a house. Where we truly dwell, divine powers join us, and the proper commentary on this is to be found not in any bibliography of Saint-Exupéry but in certain essays of Heidegger (another belated figure), or in Gaston Bachelard's *The Poetics of Space* (trans. Maria Jolas, Beacon Press, 1969).*

His conviction as to the ontological status of dwelling explains why Saint-Exupéry's repeated imagings of home-lessness and displacement are so compulsive and appalled.

* Even here there is paradox. While depicting the false condition of expatriation in the *Letter* as a double life condemned to the new but encumbered by the old, Saint-Exupéry concedes that for the heroic individual homelessness is the only authentic state, since its contingency contains the possibility of a reinvention of the self. To the intellectual, exile is freedom; it is what makes possible a sceptical style of thought. In comparable terms, Theodor Adorno in the 1950s was to castigate post-war fantasies of a return to normality:

Dwelling, in the proper sense, is now impossible. The traditional residences we have grown up in have become intolerable: each trait of comfort in them is paid for with a betrayal of knowledge, each vestige of shelter with the musty pact of family interests. The house is past [. . .]. The best mode of conduct, in the face of this, still seems an uncommitted, suspended one. It is part of morality not to be at home in one's home (*Minima Moralia*, trans. E. F. N. Jephcott, New Left Books, 1973, pp. 38–9).

To find an adequate emblem of exile, or of the communal exile that is war, he uncovers a different and negative image of the desert as a place not of life and death but of lifelessness. The desolation of an inorganic landscape, a place where nothing human has ever been, provided an insight for which Saint-Exupéry felt profoundly grateful both to the aeroplane ('[It] may just be a machine,' he writes in *Wind, Sand and Stars*, 'but what an analytical instrument it is! It has revealed to us the true face of the Earth')[7] and to his beloved Sahara. The idea that the Earth's 'naked crust' contained places as barren as anything to be found on other planets provided him with one of the limits of his thinking. An abiding image of mineral lifelessness informs his depiction of the expatriates in Lisbon as puppets, or of the anarchist militiamen in Catalonia as monstrously inert, at one with the realm of dead things surrounding them in their bunker – beyond the pale of human time. And at the moment of the little prince's most unaccommodated loneliness on Earth, when he climbs the mountain, the human planet takes on for him the undifferentiated and untenanted aspect of an asteroid among asteroids.

AUTOBIOGRAPHIES

Children's stories are often seen as unproblematically available to biographical readings. Since they are about our human origins (just as fairy tales are about our cultural infancy), the child within the story is naturally taken or mistaken for the writer-as-a-child. *The Little Prince* has been tied to the life and death of its author in unusually tenacious documentary ways, to the extent that each has been taken over by the myth of the other. The story is certainly cast in a confessional mode, and both the straying prince and the marooned airman, that other child in the story (an adult imprisoned in a childhood solitude), have been commonly interpreted as Saint-Exupéry.

'I am not sure that I have lived since childhood,' Saint-Exupéry once wrote to his mother. Cut off in adult life from the certainties of a strongly religious royalist and aristocratic upbringing, and banished from the walled garden of his own childhood paradise, he sought undoubtedly to remember, to create a memory theatre through his writings. All of his works contain highly charged accounts of childhood – and flying itself was an art of memory, triggered by hostile and threatening circumstances. In *The Little Prince* this retrospection is more controlled but also more extreme in its staging. The hero is the loneliest and most unhoused protagonist of any children's story – exiled from all normal human ties, a child with no name, without family or the concept of a family, whose own death (even if this takes the form of an apotheosis) occurs within the story rather than offstage.[8]

The Little Prince has also been read as the portrait of a marriage: the conciliatory but wayward prince as Saint-Exupéry, the petulant rose as Consuelo. In her memoir of Saint-Exupéry in America, Adèle Bréaux (who was his English tutor for several months in 1942–3, while he was living on Long Island and composing *The Little Prince*) gives a vivid account of the conjugal chaos and permanent emergency of the Saint-Exupéry household, and of the neediness of both husband and wife.[9] She also records her unguarded reaction to the sheaf of drawings which Saint-Exupéry showed her while he was at work on the story:

Something in the posture, something in the grace of the scarf and the flow of the costume, even the carriage of the little figure, reminded me of Consuelo. Something of his wife was present, a deep inescapable imprint of what he admired in her appearance.[10]

Bréaux also recalls, after the story was published, Consuelo going to a restaurant dressed up, wilfully, '*à la* little prince'.[11]

Finally, *The Little Prince* has been read as a consolation (faintly Boethian in flavour) and a double-act of leave-taking: Saint-Exupéry's farewell to his wife, prior to taking part again in the war; also, in the account of the prince's disappearance, a foreshadowing of his own mysterious end. It is as the confession of a French airman who foresees his death that the story has laid its strongest grip upon the life. *The Little Prince* was published in New York in April 1943, just as Saint-Exupéry received embarkation papers to rejoin his unit in Algeria, by which time America was committed to the war and the Allies were in North Africa. On his return he was reluctantly given leave to fly by the Gaullists whom he had done so much to annoy, but he spent much of the rest of 1943 grounded – placed on the reserve list as a result of another landing accident. By the summer of 1944 he had argued his way into the air again. On his eighth high-level reconnaissance flight, on July 31st, over the Rhône valley, he did not return; the wreckage of his plane was never discovered, nor was the cause of his disappearance ever established.

NOTES

1. In her memoir, *Saint-Exupéry in America, 1942–1943* (Fairleigh Dickinson, 1971), Adèle Bréaux describes seeing his desk covered with illustrations, while others overflowed the waste-paper basket. Many of the discarded drawings have survived, and twenty-two of these, in the collection of the Pierpont Morgan Library in New York, have recently been published for the first time in the 'Fiftieth Anniversary Edition' of *The Little Prince* (Harcourt Brace, 1993).

2. Cf. *Alice in Wonderland*:

'If everyone minded their own business,' the Duchess said, in a hoarse growl, 'the world would go round a deal faster than it does.'

'Which would not be an advantage,' said Alice, who felt very glad to get an opportunity of showing off a little of her knowledge. 'Just think what work it would make with the day and night! You see the Earth takes twenty-four hours to turn around on its axis –'

'Talking of axes,' said the Duchess, 'chop off her head!'

3. During the period of composition of *The Little Prince*, Saint-Exupéry was often consulted by the American government for his reconnaissance expertise. Adèle Bréaux (*Saint-Exupéry in America*, p. 90) recalls him describing the absurdity of this work to Paul Claudel's son when the latter visited him on Long Island:

I am frequently called to Washington without notice. I must drop my own work and take the first possible train. My business is to identify sections of Africa and the Sahara by looking at photographs taken recently from planes. My long experience as a flyer over North Africa would seem to place me in a position to recognize areas, but, in the case of the desert, the topography changes very little from one end to the other. The majority of the pictures which I scan, reveal nothing but an isolated heap of this or that in the midst of sand. It's rather useless work but I often spend two or three days at it with the hope of seeing something identifiable. I find it difficult to explain my frequent lack of success to the officials. They do not comprehend the desert's never-ending miles of sameness.

A humorous half-allusion to this experience is present in the final drawing of *The Little Prince*, a generalized cartoon image of the desert which the narrator urges his juvenile readers to commit to memory, in case they ever find themselves in the area, since this is the spot where the hero disappeared.

4. Flying over northern France, Saint-Exupéry finds a characteristically humble image for the perversion of peace that is war:

Suddenly an absurd image comes to me: stopped clocks. Every clock, stopped. Church clocks. Station clocks. Mantlepiece clocks in empty houses. The clock-maker has fled: in the window of his shop, an ossuary of dead clocks. It's war . . . no one winds the clocks. No one gathers the beetroot. No one repairs the carts (*Flight to Arras*, p. 6).

5. *Wind, Sand and Stars* (trans. W. Rees, Penguin Books, 1995), p. 38.

6. *Flight to Arras* (trans. W. Rees, Penguin Books, 1995), p. 95.

7. *Wind, Sand and Stars*, p. 31.

8. Adèle Bréaux (in *Saint-Exupéry in America*, p. 81) recalls Saint-Exupéry's words to her on this subject:

I had some trouble in persuading my publishers that the story could end with the little prince's death. *They* believe no story for children should end that way. I disagree with them. Children accept all natural things and adjust without harmful disturbances. The adults are the ones who give them wrong attitudes, who distort their notions of the natural. I don't believe that death has to be morbid. No child is going to be upset by the going of the little prince. It's just a part of things as they are.

9. See Bréaux, *Saint-Exupéry in America*.
10. Ibid., p. 75.
11. Ibid., p. 130.

FURTHER READING

Saint-Exupéry, Antoine de, Gallimard, 1953. *The Little Prince*, 'Fiftieth Anniversary Edition', Harcourt Brace, 1993.

Œuvres Complètes, vol. 1, Bibliothèque de la Pléiade, Gallimard, 1994.

Wartime Writings: 1939–1944, Harcourt Brace, 1990.

Bréaux, Adèle, *Saint-Exupéry in America, 1942–1943*, Fairleigh Dickinson, 1971.

Cate, Curtis, *Antoine de Saint-Exupéry: His Life and Times*, Heinemann, 1970.

Roy, Jules, *Saint-Exupéry*, La Manufacture, 1990.

Schiff, Stacy, *Saint-Exupéry*, Chatto & Windus, 1994.

Webster, Paul, *Antoine de Saint-Exupéry: The Life and Death of the Little Prince*, Macmillan, 1993.

TRANSLATION NOTE ON
THE LITTLE PRINCE

The Little Prince was published in New York in April 1943, in French and English, by Reynal & Hitchcock. (The unusual bilingualism of the story's publication means that the first translation, by Katherine Woods, is properly speaking as much the original work as the French text from which it was drawn.) As to the French, though Saint-Exupéry's narrator addresses children and only children, he does so in a language of conscious purity, and the translation which follows has tried to preserve something of this restraint, as being part of the story's message.

I believe that for his escape he took advantage of a flight of
migrating wild birds.

THE LITTLE PRINCE

illustrated by the author

To Léon Werth

I ask children who may read this book to forgive me for dedicating it to a grown-up. I have a genuine excuse: this grown-up is the best friend I have in the world. I have another excuse: this grown-up understands everything, even books for children. I have a third excuse: this grown-up lives in France, where he is cold and hungry. He needs a lot of consoling. If all these excuses are not enough, I will dedicate the book to the child whom this grown-up used to be, once upon a time. All grown-ups started off as children (though few of them remember). So I hereby correct my dedication:

To Léon Werth
when he was a little boy

I

Once when I was six years old I saw a magnificent picture in a book called *True Stories of the Virgin Forest*. It showed a boa constrictor swallowing a wild beast. Here is a copy of the drawing.

In the book it said: 'Boa constrictors swallow their prey whole, without chewing. Afterwards they are unable to move, and they digest by going to sleep for six months.'

This made me think a lot about the adventures of the jungle and, eventually, I succeeded with a coloured pencil in making my first drawing. My Drawing Number One. It looked like this:

I showed my masterpiece to the grown-ups, and asked if my drawing frightened them.

'Why would a hat frighten anyone?' they answered.

My drawing was not of a hat. It was of a boa constrictor digesting an elephant. So then I drew the inside of the boa constrictor, for the benefit of the grown-ups. (Grown-ups always need explanations.) My Drawing Number Two looked like this:

The grown-ups now advised me to give up drawing boa constrictors altogether, from the inside or the outside, and devote myself instead to geography, history, arithmetic and grammar. So it was that, at the age of six, I gave up a wonderful career as a painter. I had been discouraged by the failure of my Drawing Number One and my Drawing Number Two. Grown-ups never understand anything by themselves, and it is exhausting for children always and forever to be giving explanations.

I had to choose a different career, then, so I learned how to fly aeroplanes. I have flown all over the world. And geography, I will admit, has served me very well. At a glance I can distinguish China from Arizona. Which is very useful if you get lost in the night.

In the course of my life I have therefore had many dealings with many important people. I have lived a great deal among grown-ups. I have observed them from close up. This has not greatly improved my opinion of them.

Whenever I came across one who seemed to me at all clear-headed, I would try showing my Drawing Number One, which I always kept by me. I wanted to find out if this was somebody with real understanding. But the answer would always be: 'That is a hat.' In which case I would not talk to that person about boa constrictors, or virgin forests, or stars. I would place myself on their level. I would talk about bridge and golf, about politics and neckties. And the grown-up would be very pleased to have made the acquaintance of such a sensible fellow.

II

So I kept my own company, without anyone whom I could really talk to, until six years ago, when I made a forced landing in the Sahara desert. Something had broken in my engine. And as I had neither mechanic nor passengers with me, I braced myself to attempt a difficult repair job all alone. It was a matter of life or death: I had barely enough drinking water to last a week.

On the first night, then, I went to sleep on the sand a thousand miles from all human habitation. I was more isolated than a shipwrecked man on a raft in mid-ocean. So imagine my surprise to be woken at daybreak by a funny little voice saying:

'If you please – draw me a sheep!'

'What!'

'Draw me a sheep . . .'

I leapt to my feet, completely thunderstruck. I rubbed my eyes slowly. I looked around slowly. And then I saw a most extraordinary little fellow, who stood there solemnly watching me. Here is the best likeness that, later on, I was able to make of him. The drawing is certainly far less delightful than the original. But that is not my fault. I had been discouraged by the grown-ups in my career as a painter, when I was six years old, and had never learned to draw anything – except the insides of boas and the outsides of boas.

Now I was staring at this apparition before me, my eyes popping out of my head. Remember, I was a thousand miles from all human habitation. Yet this little fellow seemed neither to have lost his way, nor to be dying of exhaustion, or hunger, or thirst, or fright. Nothing about him suggested a child astray in the middle of the desert, a thousand miles from all human habitation. When I finally found my voice, I said:

'But – but what are you doing here?'

To which he merely repeated, very slowly, as though it were a matter of great consequence:

'If you please – draw me a sheep . . .'

When a mystery is too overwhelming, you do not dare to question it. Absurd as it might seem to me, a thousand

Here is the best likeness that, later on, I was able to make of
him.

miles from any inhabited place and in danger of death, I took a sheet of paper and a fountain pen out of my pocket. Then I remembered that at school I had only properly studied geography, history, arithmetic and grammar; so I told the little fellow (with a touch of irritation) that I didn't know how to draw. He replied:

'That doesn't matter. Draw me a sheep.'

As I had never drawn a sheep before, I copied out for him one of the two pictures that I did know how to draw: the boa constrictor seen from the outside.

And I was astounded to hear the little fellow say:

'No! no! no! I don't want an elephant inside a boa constrictor. Boas are very dangerous and elephants are very cumbersome. Where I come from everything is tiny. What I need is a sheep. Draw me a sheep.'

So I drew him one.

He studied it carefully. Then he said:

'No! That one is already very sickly. Do me another.'

So I drew another.

My friend smiled gently, even indulgently.

'Surely you can see for yourself – that's not a sheep; it's a ram. Look at his horns . . .'

So I did my drawing once more.

But it too was rejected, like the others:

'This one is too old. I want a sheep who will live a long time.'

My patience was by now exhausted – for I was in a hurry to start dismantling my engine – so I rapidly scribbled the drawing you see below.

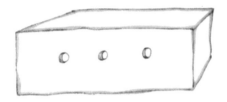

Then I added, by way of explanation:

'That is his box. The sheep you want is inside.'

And, much to my surprise, I saw the face of my young judge light up.

'That's exactly how I want him! Do you think this sheep will need a lot of grass?'

'Why?'

'Because where I come from everything is tiny.'

'Oh, there's bound to be enough. I have given you a tiny sheep.'

He bent over the drawing:

'He's not as small as all that – Look! He's gone to sleep!'

And so it was that I made the acquaintance of the little prince.

III

It took me a long time to discover where he came from. The little prince, who asked me so many questions, seemed never to hear the ones I asked him. It was from chance words, dropped here and there, that all was revealed to me. For instance, when he noticed my aeroplane for the first time (I am not going to draw my aeroplane; it would be far too complicated for me), he said:

'What is that thing over there?'

'That is not a thing. It flies. It's an aeroplane. It's my aeroplane.'

And I was proud to have him know that I could fly. At which he cried out:

'What! So you fell from the sky?'

'Yes,' I answered demurely.

'Well! How very funny . . .'

And the little prince broke into a charming peal of laughter, which I found greatly irritating. For I like my misfortunes to be taken seriously. Then he added:

'You too, then, come from the sky! Which planet are you from?'

Suddenly I had a glimmer of understanding into the mystery

of his presence here, and I quizzed him sharply:

'So you come from another planet?'

But he made no reply. He merely shook his head gently, looking all the while at my aeroplane.

'No, you can't have come very far on that thing . . .'

And he fell into a long reverie. Then, taking my drawing out of his pocket, he became absorbed in the contemplation of his treasure.

You can imagine how intrigued I was by this half-confidence about 'other planets'. I did my utmost, therefore, to find out more.

'Where are you from, then, little fellow? Where is this "where I live" that you mention? Where do you want to take my sheep?'

After a reflective silence, he answered:

'The best thing about the box you've given me is that at night he can use it as his house.'

'Of course. And if you are good, I will give you a rope to tether him with during the day. And a post to tether him to.'

This proposal seemed to shock the little prince.

'Tether him? What an odd idea!'

'But if you don't tether him, he may go anywhere and end up lost.'

And my friend burst out laughing once more.

'But where do you imagine he would go?'

'Anywhere. Straight ahead of him.'

At which the little prince remarked solemnly:

'That won't matter; where I come from it's so very small!'

Then, with perhaps a hint of sadness, he added:

'Straight ahead does not take anyone very far . . .'

IV

From this I learned a second fact of great importance: the planet he came from was scarcely bigger than a house!

This was no great surprise to me. I knew very well that, besides the important planets – Earth, Jupiter, Mars, Venus, and so on – to which names have been given, there are also hundreds of others, some so small that one has trouble finding them even through the telescope. When an astronomer discovers one of these, he gives it a number instead of a name. So he might call it, for instance, 'Asteroid 3251'.

I have good reason to believe that the planet from which the little prince came is the asteroid known as B 612. This asteroid has only once been seen through the telescope: by a Turkish astronomer, in 1909.

At the time, this astronomer made a grand presentation of his discovery before an International Congress of Astronomy. But since he was wearing Turkish national costume nobody would believe him. Grown-ups are like that . . .

Fortunately for the reputation of Asteroid

The little prince on Asteroid B 612.

B 612, a Turkish dictator ordered his subjects, on pain of death, to convert to European dress. In 1920 our astronomer repeated his demonstration, wearing elegant evening dress. This time everyone accepted his proofs.

The reason I have told you so much about Asteroid B 612, and let you know its number, is because of grown-ups. Grown-ups love figures. When you describe a new friend to them, they never ask you about the important things. They never say: 'What's his voice like? What are his favourite games? Does he collect butterflies?' Instead they demand: 'How old is he? How many brothers has he? How much does he weigh? How much does his father earn?' Only then do they feel they know him. If you say to the grown-ups: 'I've seen a lovely house made of pink brick, with geraniums in the windows and doves on the roof', they are unable to picture such a house. You

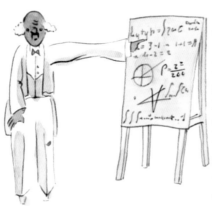

must say: 'I saw a house that cost a hundred thousand francs.' Then they cry out: 'Oh, how pretty!'

Again, you might say to them: 'The proof that the little prince existed is that he was enchanting, that he laughed, and that he was looking for a sheep. When someone wants a sheep, it is proof that they exist.' The grown-ups will merely shrug their shoulders, and treat you like a child. But if you tell them: 'The planet he came from is Asteroid B 612', then they will be convinced, and will spare you all their questions. That is how they are. You must not hold it against them. Children have to be very indulgent towards grown-ups.

Of course, for we who understand life, figures are quite unimportant. I would have liked to begin this story in the manner of a fairy tale. I would have liked to write:

'Once upon a time there was a little prince who lived on a planet scarcely bigger than himself, and who was in need of a friend . . .' To those who understand life, that would have a much greater air of truth.

You see, I do not want my story to be taken lightly. I have suffered so much grief setting down these memories. Already six years have passed since my friend went away, along with his sheep. If I try to describe him here, it is so as not to forget him. To forget a friend is sad. Not everyone has had a friend. And if I do forget him, I might become like those grown-ups who no longer care for anything except figures.

It is for this reason, too, that I have bought a paintbox and some pencils. It is hard to take up drawing again at my age, when the only attempts you have ever made were of the boa constrictor from the outside and the boa constrictor from the inside, when you were six years old! Of course, I shall try to make my portraits as true to life as I can. But I am not at all sure of succeeding. Some drawings work, others do not. Sometimes my proportions are wrong: here the little prince is too big; there he is too little. Other times I waver over the colour of his clothes. And so I fumble along, trying this and that, as best I can. I may even make mistakes as to more important details. But there you must forgive me. You see, my friend never gave explanations. Perhaps he thought I was like him. But I, unfortunately, am not able to see sheep through the walls of boxes. Perhaps I am a bit of a grown-up after all. I must be getting old.

V

Each day I learned something about the little prince's planet, his departure from it, his journey. The details came very slowly, in the course of conversation. So it was, on the third day, that I learned about the terrible baobabs.

This time, once again, I had the sheep to thank. For, abruptly – as if seized by grave doubts – the little prince demanded:

'It is true, isn't it, that sheep eat small bushes?'

'Yes. It is true.'

'Good! I am glad!'

I could not see why it was so important that sheep should eat small bushes. But the little prince added:

'Then it follows that they also eat baobabs?'

I reminded the little

prince that baobabs are not small bushes but trees the size of churches; and that even if he took a whole herd of elephants home with him, they would not succeed in dispatching a single baobab.

The idea of the herd of elephants made the little prince laugh.

'They would have to be stacked on top of each other.'

Then he observed, wisely enough:

'Baobabs, before they grow big, start off small.'

'So they do. But why do you want your sheep to eat up the baby baobabs?'

He merely replied: 'Oh, come, come', as if it went without saying. And I had to make a great mental effort to work out the problem on my own.

In effect, there were on the little prince's planet, as on every planet, good plants and bad plants. And consequently there were good seeds from good plants, and bad seeds from bad plants. But seeds, as everyone knows, are invisible. They sleep in the secrecy of the earth, until one of them suddenly decides to wake up. So it stretches itself and, timidly at first, extends towards the sun a ravishing, inno-cent little shoot. If this happens to be a sprig of radish, or the beginnings of a rose bush, you can leave it to grow wherever it wishes. But if it turns out to be a bad plant, you must root it up at once, the very instant you recognize it. Now there were some terrible seeds on the little prince's planet – namely those of the baobab tree. The soil of the planet was infested with them. And a baobab, if you tackle it too late, can never be got rid of afterwards. It clutters everything. It will bore right through a planet with its roots. And if the planet is too small, and if the baobabs are too numerous, they will finally make the planet explode.

'It's a question of discipline,' the little prince informed me later on. 'When you finish washing and dressing each morning, you must carefully wash and dress your planet. You must force yourself to pull up the baobabs regularly, as soon as they can be distinguished from the rose trees – which they resemble so closely in early youth. It is very tedious work, but it is very easy.'

And one day he suggested that I set about making a

The baobabs.

beautiful drawing, so as to give children on my planet a clear idea of all this. 'Then, if one day they travel,' he said, 'that will be of use to them. Sometimes one can safely put off what needs doing until later. But in the case of baobabs it always ends in disaster. I knew a planet that was inhabited by a lazy fellow. He neglected three little bushes, and guess what happened . . .'

So, following the little prince's directions, I have made a drawing of that planet. I don't much like adopting the tone of a moralist. But the peril of baobabs is so little understood, and the risks run by anyone who strays on to an asteroid are so considerable, that for once I will break my usual reserve, and say categorically: 'Children! Beware of baobabs!'

It is to warn friends of a danger they have skirted unknowingly for too long, as I myself have done, that I worked so hard at this drawing. The lesson I had to pass on was worth the trouble it has cost me. Perhaps you are asking yourselves: why are there no other drawings in this book as magnificent as the baobab drawing? The answer is quite simple: I tried with the rest, but did not succeed. When I drew the baobabs I was driven on by a sense of urgency.

VI

Ah, little prince! So it was, gradually, that I came to understand your melancholy little life! For a long time your only pleasure had been to watch the gently setting sun. I learned this new detail on the morning of the fourth day, when you said to me:

'I am very fond of sunsets. Let's go this moment and look at a sunset.'

'But we shall have to wait . . .'

'Wait for what?'

'Wait until it's time for the sun to set.'

At first you seemed very taken aback. Then you laughed at yourself and said:

'I still keep thinking I'm at home!'

Just so. For as everyone knows, when it is noon in the United States the sun is setting over France. If you could get to France in a twinkling, you could watch a sunset right now. Unfortunately France is rather too far away. But on your tiny planet, little prince, you had only to move your chair a few steps. You could watch night fall whenever you liked.

'One day,' you said, 'I watched the sunset forty-three times!'

And a little later you added:

'You know, when one is that sad, one can get to love the sunset.'

'Were you that sad, then, on the day of the forty-three sunsets?'

But the prince made no answer.

VII

On the fifth day – thanks to the sheep, as always – the secret of the little prince's life was finally revealed to me. Without preamble, as though voicing aloud a problem he had long meditated in silence, he abruptly asked:

'If a sheep eats small bushes, will it therefore eat flowers?'

'A sheep eats everything in its path.'

'Even flowers with thorns?'

'Yes. Even flowers with thorns.'

'So what's the use of thorns?'

I did not know the answer. At that moment I was busy trying to unscrew a bolt that had got stuck in my engine. I was very worried, for my breakdown was beginning to look fairly serious, and the low reserves of drinking water made me fear the worst.

'So what's the use of thorns?'

The little prince never gave up on a question once he had asked it. I was irritated with my bolt, so I said the first thing that entered my head:

'Thorns are of no use whatsoever; they are simply a flower's way of being spiteful!'

'Oh!'

There was a silence; then he retorted, with a kind of bitterness:

'I don't believe you! Flowers are weak, they are naive. They reassure them- selves as best they can. They think they are being frighten- ing, with their thorns.'

I made no answer. At that moment I was saying to myself: 'If this bolt resists any longer, I am going to knock it out with the hammer.' The little prince interrupted my thoughts once more:

'But as for you, you think that the flowers . . .'

'Not at all! Not at all! I think nothing! I told you the first thing that entered my head. As for me, I happen to have serious matters to attend to!'

He stared at me in amazement.

'Serious matters!'

He looked at me, hammer in hand, fingers black with grease, bent over some machine that seemed to him merely ugly.

'You are talking like a grown-up!'

This made me feel a little ashamed. But he continued, relentlessly:

'You are confusing everything . . . you are mixing up everything!'

He was truly very angry. He was shaking his golden locks in the breeze.

'I know a planet where a certain purple-faced gentleman lives. He has never inhaled the scent of a flower. He has never looked at a star. He has never loved anyone. He has never done anything except add up figures. And all day long, just like you, he repeats to himself: "I am a serious person! I am a serious person!" And this makes him swell up with pride. But he is not a man – he's a mushroom!'

'A what?'

'A mushroom!'

The little prince was now quite pale with anger.

'For millions of years flowers have been growing thorns. For millions of years sheep have been eating flowers none the less. And is it not a serious matter, to try and understand why flowers go to such trouble producing thorns that will never be of any use to them? Is it not important, the war between sheep and flowers? Is it not more serious and more important than the calculations of a fat red-faced gentleman? And if I personally know a flower which is unique in the world, which exists nowhere except on my planet, but which one little sheep can destroy in a single bite, just like that, one morning, without even noticing what he's doing – well, I suppose that, too, is of no importance!'

He flushed, then continued:

'If someone loves a flower, of which there is only one example among all the millions and millions of stars, that is enough to make him happy when he looks up at the night sky. He says to himself: "Somewhere out there is my flower." But if a sheep eats the flower, it's as though all the stars have suddenly gone out! But I suppose that, too, is of no importance!'

He could not say any more. His words were choked by sobbing. Night had fallen. I had let my tools drop to the ground. I no longer cared a fig for my hammer, or my bolt, or about thirst or about dying. On one star, one planet, this planet, the Earth, there was a little prince in need of consoling! I took him in my arms. I cradled him. I told him: 'The flower you love is not in danger . . . I'll draw you a muzzle for your sheep . . . I'll draw you a shield to put round your flower . . . I'll . . .' I did not really know what to say. I felt like a blundering idiot. I did not know how to reach him, where to catch up with him. It is such a secret place, the land of tears.

VIII

I soon learned to know more about this flower.

The flowers on the little prince's planet had always been very straightforward. Adorned with just a single row of petals, they took up no room and troubled nobody. They would appear one morning in the grass, only to fade away in the evening. But one day a very particular flower had sprung up, from a seed blown from who knows where; and the little prince had kept a close eye on this shoot, which was so unlike the others. After all, it might have been a new strain of baobab.

But the shrub soon stopped growing and started getting ready to produce a flower. The little prince watched the growth of an enormous bud, convinced that some miraculous apparition must follow. Closeted in her green room, however, this flower took an age preparing herself to be beautiful. She chose her colours with care. She dressed slowly, adjusting her petals one by one. She did not want to come into the world all crumpled, like the field poppies; she wanted to appear only in the full radiance of her beauty. That's right! She was very stylish! Her mysterious preparations lasted for days and days. Then one morning, exactly at sunrise, she suddenly revealed herself.

And after labouring with such painstaking precision, she merely said with a yawn:

'Oh! I am scarcely awake . . . You must excuse me . . . I'm still all dishevelled . . .'

At this the little prince could not contain his admiration:

'But you are so beautiful!'

'Aren't I, just?' replied the flower, sweetly. 'And to think I was born at the same moment as the sun . . .'

The little prince soon guessed that this flower was none too modest – but how thrilling she was!

'Surely it must be time for breakfast,' she announced shortly. 'Would you be so kind as to attend to me?'

And the little prince, all flustered, fetched a watering can of cool water and proceeded to wait upon the flower.

From the beginning, then, she began to torment him with her somewhat touchy vanity. One day, for example, talking about her four thorns, she said to the little prince:

'Let them come, the tigers, with their claws!'

'There are no tigers on my planet,' the little prince inter-rupted. 'In any case – tigers do not eat weeds.'

'I am not a weed,' the flower murmured sweetly.

'Forgive me . . .'

'Nor am I in the least afraid of tigers, but I do have a

horror of draughts. You wouldn't happen to have a screen to hand?'

'A horror of draughts? That is
bad luck, for a plant,' the little
prince remarked, and
added to himself, 'This
flower is very compli-
cated.'

'In the evenings you
may place a glass dome
over me. It is very cold
on your planet. It lacks
conveniences. Where I
come from —'

Here she interrupted herself. For she had come in the
shape of a seed, and could not possibly know anything
about other worlds. Ashamed at letting herself be caught
on the verge of such a naive
lie, she coughed two or
three times, to make
the little prince feel at
fault.

'About that screen . . .?'

'I was going to fetch it, but
you were talking to me!'

At which she pretended to
cough once more, so that
he might suffer some
remorse just
the same.

So it was that the little prince, despite the willing nature of his love, had soon come to doubt his flower. He had taken at face value her words of no importance, and they made him very unhappy.

'I should not have listened to her,' he confided to me one day. 'You must never listen to flowers. You must simply gaze at them and breathe them in. My flower perfumed my whole planet, but I was unable to appreciate her. All that nonsense about claws, which I found so irritating, ought to have endeared her to me.'

He continued his confidences:

'In those days I understood nothing! I should have judged by her deeds and not her words. She cast her fragrance around me and brightened my life. I should never have run away! I should have guessed the tenderness behind her poor little stratagems. Flowers are so contradictory! And I was too young to know how to love her.'

IX

I believe that for his escape he took advantage of a flight of migrating wild birds. On the morning of his departure he set his planet in good order. He carefully swept out his active volcanoes. He had two active volcanoes – which were very useful for heating up breakfast in the mornings. He also had an extinct volcano. But, as he used to say: 'One never knows!' So he swept out the extinct volcano, too. If they are well swept, volcanoes burn slowly and steadily, without erupting. Volcanic eruptions are like chimney fires. Here on Earth we are, of course, far too small to sweep out our volcanoes. Which is why they cause us endless trouble.

With a feeling of sadness, the little prince then uprooted the last little shoots of baobab. He was thinking he might never return here. And on this last morning the familiar tasks all seemed very precious to him. So that when he watered his flower for the last time, and prepared to place her under her glass dome, he found that he was on the verge of tears.

'Goodbye,' he said to the flower.

But she did not reply.

'Goodbye,' he repeated.

The flower coughed. But this was not on account of her cold.

'I have been an idiot,' she said to him at last. 'I ask your forgiveness. Try to be happy.'

He was taken aback by this absence of reproaches. He

He carefully swept out his active volcanoes.

stood there all disconcerted, the glass dome suspended in mid-air. He could not understand this sweet composure of hers.

'Yes, yes, of course I love you,' the flower said to him at last. 'You had no idea – which is my fault. It is of no consequence. But you have been as foolish as I. Try to be happy. And leave that glass alone, I don't want it any more.'

'But what about the wind?'

'My cold is not as bad as all that . . . The cool night air will do me good. I am a flower.'

'But what about insects?'

'I'll simply have to put up with two or three caterpillars if I want to meet some butterflies. I have heard that they are very beautiful. Otherwise, who will visit me? You will be far away. As for wild animals, I am not afraid of them. I have my claws.'

And she innocently showed her four thorns. Then she added:

'Don't hang about like that, it's irritating. You've decided to go. Now go!'

For she did not want him to see her tears. She was such a haughty flower . . .

X

He found himself in the vicinity of Asteroids 325, 326, 327, 328, 329 and 330. So he started by visiting these, to find some occupation and to educate himself.

The first was inhabited by a king. Clad in purple and

ermine, the king was in sitting – on a very simple yet majestic throne.

'Ah! Here comes a subject,' exclaimed the king when he caught sight of the little prince.

And the little prince said to himself:

'How can he recognize me, when he has never seen me before?'

The little prince did not realize that for kings the world is very simple: all men are subjects.

'Come nearer, so that I may see you better,' said the king, who felt very proud at last to be a king in the eyes of somebody.

The little prince looked around him quickly for somewhere to sit, but the entire planet was taken up by the king's magnificent ermine robe. So he remained standing, and, because he was tired, he yawned.

'It is contrary to etiquette to yawn in the presence of a king,' said the monarch. 'I forbid you to yawn.'

'I can't help myself,' replied the little prince, quite abashed. 'I have had a long journey, and have not slept.'

'In which case,' said the king, 'I command you to yawn. It is years since I have seen anyone yawning. Yawns are, to me, an object of curiosity. Hurry up! Yawn again. That is a command.'

'Now I feel intimidated . . . I can't, just at the moment . . .' murmured the little prince, going very red in the face.

'H'm! H'm!' replied the king. 'In that case I – I command you sometimes to yawn and at other times to . . .'

He muttered something, and seemed put out.

For what this king fundamentally insisted upon was that his authority be respected. He would not tolerate disobedience. He was an absolute monarch. At the same time, since

at heart he was a very good man, he made his commands
reasonable.

'Were I,' he would often say, 'were I to command a
general to change into a sea-bird, and were this general not
to obey, it would not be the general's fault. It would be my
fault.'

'May I sit down?' the little prince now
enquired timidly.

'I command you to sit down,' replied
the king, majestically drawing in a fold of his ermine mantle.

The little prince was astonished. This planet was minuscule. Over what, precisely, could the king be said to reign?

'Sire,' he said, 'I beg to be excused for asking you a question –'

'I command you to ask me a question,' the king interjected hurriedly.

'Sire, over what do you reign?'

'Over everything,' replied the king, with huge simplicity.

'Over everything?'

With a quiet gesture the king indicated his planet, the other planets, and all the stars.

'Over all that?' asked the prince.

'Over all that,' replied the king.

For not only was he an absolute monarch, he was a universal monarch.

'And do the stars obey you?'

'Naturally,' said the king. 'They obey promptly. I do not tolerate indiscipline.'

The little prince marvelled at such power. Had he wielded it himself, he'd have been able to sit and watch, nor forty-four sunsets in a single day, but seventy-two, even a hundred, even two hundred, without ever having to move his chair! And, since at the thought of his little forsaken planet he felt himself becoming sad, he plucked up courage to ask a favour of the king:

'I would like to see a sunset . . . Do me this kindness: command the sun to set.'

'Were I to command a general to fly from one flower to the next, like a butterfly, or to write a tragedy, or to change into a sea-bird, and were this general not to carry out my command, which of us would be in the wrong – he or I?'

'You would be,' said the little prince firmly.

'Correct. One must require of each what each is able to give,' continued the king. 'Authority rests first of all upon reason. If you command your subjects to go and throw themselves into the sea, there will be a revolution. I have the right to demand obedience because my orders are reasonable.'

'And my sunset?' the little prince reminded him, for he never forgot a question once he had asked it.

'You shall have your sunset. I shall insist upon it. But I shall wait, in keeping with my science of government, until conditions are favourable.'

'When will that be?' enquired the little prince.

'H'm! H'm!' replied the king, consulting an outsized almanac. 'H'm! H'm! That will be at around . . . around . . . That will be this evening, at around twenty minutes to eight! Then you shall see how I'm obeyed.'

The little prince yawned. He was regretting his missed sunset. And he was already beginning to be a little bored.

'I have nothing further to do here,' he said to the king. 'So I'll be on my way!'

'Don't leave,' replied the king, who was very proud at having a subject. 'Don't leave, I shall make you a Minister!'

'Minister of what?'

'Of – of Justice!'

'But there is nobody here to judge!'

'We do not know for certain,' said the king. 'I have not yet made a complete tour of my kingdom. I am very old. There is no room here for a state coach, and it tires me to walk.'

'But I have already looked!' said the little prince, bending again to glance around the other side of the planet. 'There's no one over there either.'

'In that case, you shall judge yourself,' replied the king. 'That is the most difficult thing of all. It is far more difficult to judge oneself than to judge others. If you succeed in judging yourself correctly, then you are truly a man of wisdom.'

'But I can judge myself anywhere,' said the little prince. 'I do not need to live on this planet.'

'H'm! H'm!' said the king. 'I do believe that somewhere on my planet there is an old rat. I hear him at night. You may judge this old rat. From time to time you will condemn him to death. Hence his life will depend on your justice. But you will reprieve him each time, so as to save him up. He's the only one we have.'

'But I don't like condemning to death,' said the little prince, 'and I really do think I should be going now.'

'No,' said the king.

Having completed his preparations, but with no wish to distress the old monarch, the little prince said:

'If Your Majesty wishes to be obeyed promptly, he might give me a reasonable command. He might, for example, command me to leave within the next minute. It seems to me that conditions are favourable.'

As the king made no reply, the little prince hesitated; then, with a sigh, he took his leave.

'I make you my Ambassador,' the king cried out hurriedly after him.

He had a wonderful air of authority.

'Grown-ups are very strange,' the little prince said to himself, as he continued on his voyage.

XI

The second planet was inhabited by a conceited man.

'Ah! Ah! Here comes an admirer to visit me,' cried out the conceited man, from afar, as soon as he caught sight of the little prince. For, to the conceited man, all other men are admirers.

'Good day,' said the little prince. 'That's a funny hat you're wearing.'

'It's for waving with,' replied the conceited man. 'For waving with when people cheer me. Unfortunately, nobody ever passes this way.'

'Oh really?' said the little prince, who did not really understand.

'Clap your hands, one against the other,' the conceited man now instructed him.

The little prince clapped his hands, one against the other. And the conceited man raised his hat and waved modestly.

'This is more amusing than my visit to the king,' the little prince said to himself. And he started clapping his hands again, one against the other. And the conceited man raised his hat and waved.

After five minutes of this exercise the little prince grew tired of the monotony of the game.

'And for you to lower your hat,' he asked, 'what do I have to do?'

But the conceited man did not hear him. Conceited men only ever hear praise.

'Do you really admire me a great deal?' he asked the little prince.

'What does "admire" mean?'

'To admire means to admit that I am the handsomest, the best-dressed, the richest, the most intelligent person on this planet.'

'But you are all alone on your planet!'

'Do me this kindness: admire me all the same!'

'I admire you,' said the prince, with a slight shrug of his shoulders, 'but how can that be of any interest to you?'

And the little prince went away.

'Grown-ups are decidedly very odd,' he merely observed to himself, as he continued on his voyage.

XII

The next planet was inhabited by a drinker. This visit was very short, but it plunged the little prince into a deep melancholy.

'What are you doing there?' he said to the drinker, whom he found settled silently before a collection of empty bottles and a collection of full bottles.

'I'm drinking,' said the drinker, with a mournful air.

'Why are you drinking?' asked the little prince.

'To forget,' replied the drinker.

'To forget what?' enquired the little prince, who was already starting to feel sorry for him.

'To forget that I'm ashamed,' confessed the drinker, hanging his head.

'Ashamed of what?' persisted the little prince, who wanted to help him.

'Ashamed of drinking!' concluded the drinker, retreating into permanent silence.

And the little prince went away, perplexed.

'Grown-ups are decidedly very, very odd,' he said to himself, as he continued on his voyage.

XIII

The fourth planet belonged to a businessman. This man was so busy that he did not even raise his head at the little prince's arrival.

'Good day,' said the latter. 'Your cigarette has gone out.'

'Three and two make five. Five and seven make twelve. Twelve and three make fifteen. Good day. Fifteen and seven make twenty-two. Twenty-two and six make twenty-eight. I've no time to relight it. Twenty-six and five make thirty-one. Phew! That makes five-hundred-and-one million six-hundred-and-twenty-two thousand seven-hundred-and-thirty-one.'

'Five hundred million what?'

'Eh? Are you still there? Five-hundred-and-one million . . . I can't remember what. I have too much to do! I happen to be a serious person, I've no time for idle chatter! Two and five make seven . . .'

'Five-hundred-and-one-million what?' repeated the little prince, who had never in his life given up on a question once he had asked it.

The businessman raised his head.

'During the fifty-four years I have lived on this planet, I have been disturbed on only three occasions. The first was twenty-two years ago, when some May-bug dropped from heaven knows where. He made the most dreadful din that resounded all over the place, and I made four mistakes in my addition. The second time was eleven years ago, brought on by an attack of rheumatism. I need exercise. I have no time for sauntering about. The third time – the third is standing right in front of me now! As I was saying, then, five-hundred-and-one million . . .'

'Millions of what?'

The businessman could see there was no hope of being left in peace.

'Millions of those small objects you sometimes see up in the sky.'

'Flies?'

'No, no, no. Small glittering objects.'

'Bees?'

'No, no, no. Small gilded objects that set idle minds daydreaming. Though I, for my part, happen to be a serious person! I've no time for daydreaming.'

'Ah! You mean stars?'

'Just so. Stars.'

'And what can you do with five hundred million stars?'

'Five-hundred-and-one million six-hundred-and-twenty-two thousand seven-hundred-and-thirty-one. I happen to be a serious person, a precise person.'

'And what do you do with these stars?'

'Do with them?'

'Yes.'

'Nothing. I own them.'

'You own the stars?'

'Yes.'

'But I have just seen a king who –'

'Kings do not "own". Kings "reign over". There is a large difference.'

'And of what use is it to you to own the stars?'

'Its use is to make me rich.'

'And of what use is it to you to be rich?'

'To buy more stars, if there are any more to be discovered.'

'This fellow,' the little prince said to himself, 'reasons a little like my drunkard.'

Nevertheless, he had a few more questions to ask:

'How can you own the stars?'

'To whom do they belong?' snapped the businessman peevishly.

'I don't know. To nobody.'

'Then they belong to me, since I thought of it first.'

'Is that all it takes?'

'Naturally. When you find a diamond that belongs to nobody, it belongs to you. When you discover an island that belongs to nobody, it belongs to you. When you are the first to have an idea, you take out a patent on it: it belongs to you. And the stars belong to me, because nobody before me ever thought of owning them.'

'That much is true,' said the little prince. 'And what do you do with them?'

'I administer them. I count them and I recount them,' said the businessman. 'It is hard work. But then I happen to be a serious person!'

The little prince was still not satisfied.

'If I own a scarf,' he said, 'I can put it round my neck and take it with me. If I own a flower, I can gather my flower and take it with me. But you cannot gather the stars!'

'No, but I can deposit them in the bank.'

'What does that mean?'

'It means that I write down the number of stars I own on a piece of paper. Then I lock this paper up in a drawer.'

'And is that all?'

'That is enough!'

'It is amusing,' thought the little prince. 'It is even rather poetic. But it's not terribly serious.'

About serious things, the little prince had very different ideas to those of grown-ups.

'I myself own a flower,' he persisted, 'which I water every day. I own three volcanoes, which I sweep out every week (for I also sweep out the extinct volcano: one never knows). It is of use to my volcanoes, and it is of use to my flower, that I own them. But you are of no use to the stars.'

The businessman opened his mouth, but found nothing to say in answer, and the little prince went away.

'Grown-ups are decidedly altogether extraordinary,' he merely said to himself, as he continued on his voyage.

XIV

The fifth planet was very strange. It was the smallest of all. There was just enough room to accommodate a street lamp and a lamplighter. The little prince could not imagine what use there might be, somewhere in the heavens, on a planet with neither houses nor people, for a street lamp and a lamplighter. But he said to himself:

'This man may well be absurd. Nevertheless, he's not as absurd as the king, or the conceited man, or the businessman, or the drinker. At least his work has some meaning. When he lights up his street lamp, it's as though he were bringing a new star to life, or a flower. When he puts out his street lamp, he is putting the flower or the star to sleep. It is a beautiful occupation. And, since it is beautiful, it is truly useful.'

When he touched down on this planet he respectfully greeted the lamplighter:

'Good day. Why have you just extinguished your street lamp?'

'Those are the orders,' replied the lamplighter. 'Good morning.'

'What are orders?'

'Orders are to extinguish my lamp. Good evening.'

And he lit it again.

'But why have you just lit up again?'

'Those are the orders,' replied the lamplighter.

'I don't understand,' said the little prince.

'There's nothing to understand,' said the lamplighter. 'Orders are orders. Good morning.'

'It's a terrible way to earn a living.'

And he extinguished his street lamp.

Then he mopped his forehead with a red-check hand-kerchief.

'It's a terrible way to earn a living. In the old days it was reasonable. I extinguished in the morning and lit up in the evening. I had the rest of the day for relaxing, and the rest of the night for sleeping.'

'And since that time the orders have changed?'

'The orders have not changed,' said the lamplighter. 'That is the tragedy of it! Year by year the planet has been revolving more and more rapidly, but the orders have not changed!'

'So?'

'So now it completes one revolution every minute, and I no longer have a moment's rest. I light up and extinguish once every minute!'

'How very funny! The days on your planet last just one minute!'

'It's not in the least funny,' said the lamplighter. 'A month has already gone by since we started talking.'

'A month?'

'Yes. Thirty minutes. Thirty days! Good evening.'

And he relit his lamp.

As he watched, the little prince felt drawn to this lamplighter who was so faithful to orders. He remembered the sunsets he used himself to seek out, in earlier days, simply by pulling up his chair. He wanted to help this new friend.

'You know, I can think of a way you could rest whenever you wanted to.'

'I always want to rest,' said the lamplighter.

(For it is possible for someone to be faithful and lazy at the same time.)

The little prince continued:

'Your planet is so small that three strides will take you all the way around it. You have only to walk slowly enough, and you can remain in daylight all the time. When you want to rest, you simply walk – and the day will last as long as you like.'

'That does not get me very far,' said the lamplighter. 'What I like doing in life is sleeping.'

'That is bad luck,' said the little prince.

'It is bad luck,' said the lamplighter. 'Good morning.'

And he extinguished his lamp.

'This fellow,' said the little prince to himself, as he continued on his travels, 'would be laughed at by all the others: by the king, by the conceited man, by the drinker, by the businessman. However, he is the only one who does not seem to me ridiculous. Perhaps that is because he is preoccupied with something other than himself.'

He breathed a sigh of regret and went on thinking:

'He is the only one I could have made my friend. But his planet is altogether too small. There's no room for two of us.'

What the little prince did not like to admit was that he was sorry to leave this planet most of all because it was blessed with one-thousand-four-hundred-and-forty sunsets every twenty-four hours!

XV

The sixth planet was ten times larger than the previous one. It was inhabited by an old gentleman who wrote voluminous books.

'Well, well! Here comes an explorer!' he exclaimed to himself when he caught sight of the little prince.

The little prince sat down on the table and panted a little. He had already travelled so very far!

'Where do you come from?' said the old gentleman.

'What is that big book?' said the little prince. 'What do you do here?'

'I am a geographer,' said the old gentleman.

'What is a geographer?'

'A geographer is a learned man who knows where all the seas, rivers, towns, mountains and deserts are located.'

'Now that is interesting,' said the little prince. 'Here is a real profession, at last!' And he looked around him at the geographer's planet. Never before had he seen so magnificent a planet.

'It is certainly beautiful, your planet. Does it have oceans?'

'I can't tell,' said the geographer.

'Ah!' (The little prince was disappointed.) 'And mountains?'

'I can't tell,' said the geographer.

'And towns and rivers and deserts?'

'I can't tell you that either,' said the geographer.

'But you're a geographer!'

'Quite so,' said the geographer. 'But I am not an explorer. I am in dire need of explorers. It is not the geographer's job to go around counting off the towns, the rivers, the mountains, the seas, the oceans and the deserts. The geographer is far too important to go sauntering about. He does not leave his desk. But there he sits and receives the explorers. He asks them questions, and he notes down what they recollect of their travels. And if the recollections of any of them seem interesting, the geographer will order an inquiry into the moral character of the explorer concerned.'

'Why is that?'

'Because an explorer who told lies would cause havoc with the geography books. So would an explorer who drank too much.'

'Why is that?' said the little prince.

'Because drunkards see double. So the geographer would

record two mountains in a place where there is only one.'

'I know somebody,' said the little prince, 'who would make a bad explorer.'

'I can well believe it. Then, when the explorer's morals are shown to be sound, we hold an inquiry into his discovery.'

'Someone goes and looks?'

'No. That would be too complicated. Instead we require the explorer to furnish proofs. For example, if the discovery in question is that of a large mountain, we require him to bring back some large stones.'

The geographer suddenly became excited.

'But you, for example, you come from far away! You are an explorer! You can describe your planet to me!'

And, opening his register, the geographer began to sharpen his pencil. For the narratives of explorers are entered first in pencil. Before they can be entered in ink the explorer must furnish proofs.

'Well?' said the geographer expectantly.

'Oh, where I come from is not very interesting,' said the little prince. 'Everything is so small. I have three volcanoes. Two are active and the third is extinct. But one never knows.'

'One never knows,' said the geographer.

'I also have a flower.'

'We do not take note of flowers,' said the geographer.

'Whyever not! They're prettier than everything else!'

'Because flowers are ephemeral.'

'What does "ephemeral" mean?'

'Geography books,' said the geographer, 'are the most precious of all books. They never go out of date. It is very rare for a mountain to change position. It is very rare for an ocean to be emptied of its water. We record what is eternal.'

'But extinct volcanoes can come back to life,' the little prince interrupted. 'What does "ephemeral" mean?'

'Whether volcanoes are dead or alive, it amounts to the same as far as we are concerned,' said the geographer. 'What counts for us is the mountain. And that does not change.'

'But what does "ephemeral" mean?' repeated the little prince, who had never in his whole life given up on a question once he had asked it.

'It means: "which is threatened with impending death".'

'My flower is threatened with impending death?'

'Certainly.'

'My flower is ephemeral,' the little prince said to himself, 'and she has only four thorns to defend herself against the world! And I have left her all alone on my planet!'

It was his first impulse of regret. But he took heart again.

'What do you recommend me to visit next?' he asked.

'The planet Earth,' replied the geographer. 'It has a good reputation . . .'

And the little prince went away, thinking of his flower.

XVI

So the seventh planet he visited was the Earth.

The Earth is not just any old planet. Its inhabitants number one-hundred-and-eleven kings (not forgetting, of course, the Negro kings), seven thousand geographers, nine hundred thousand businessmen, seven-and-a-half million drunks, three-hundred-and-eleven million conceited men . . . In other words, approximately two billion grown-ups.

To give you an idea of the size of the Earth, I can tell you that before the invention of electricity it was necessary to maintain, over the whole of the six continents, a veritable army of four-hundred-and-sixty-two thousand five-hundred-and-eleven lamplighters.

Seen from not so high up, the effect was very splendid. The movements of this army were regulated like the ballet in an opera. First came the turn of the lamplighters of New Zealand and Australia. Having lit their lanterns, they would then go off to sleep. Next in the dance, the lamplighters of China and Siberia entered on cue. Then they too were conjured off into the wings. Then came the turn of the lamplighters of Russia and the Indies. Then those of Africa and Europe. Then those of South America. Then those of North America. And never did they mistake their order of appearance on stage. It was an imposing spectacle.

Only the man in charge of the single street lamp on the North Pole, and his colleague in charge of the single street lamp on the South Pole, used to lead lives of careless indolence: these two went to work only twice a year.

XVII

When you are trying to be witty, you are apt sometimes to wander from the truth. I have not been altogether honest in describing the lamplighters. I realize that I am in danger of giving a false impression of our planet to those who are not acquainted with it. Mankind takes up very little space on Earth. If the two billion inhabitants who populate the Earth were to stand up and squeeze fairly close together, as if for a public meeting, they could easily be accommodated on a public square twenty miles long and twenty miles wide. You could cram humanity on to the least little islet of the Pacific.

Grown-ups, of course, will not believe you when you tell them this. They think they take up a lot of space. They fancy themselves as important as the baobabs. You must therefore suggest they do the calculation for themselves. They adore figures: it will make them happy. But don't waste your time on this chore. It is pointless. Believe me.

After arriving on Earth, the little prince was very surprised not to see any people. He was beginning to fear he had come to the wrong planet, when something coil-shaped, the colour of moonlight, stirred in the sand before him.

'Good evening,' said the little prince, just in case.

'Good evening,' said the snake.

'What planet have I landed on?' asked the little prince.

'On Earth, in Africa,' the snake replied.

'Ah! . . . So there are no people on the Earth?'

'Here it is the desert. There are no people in the desert. The Earth is large,' said the snake.

The little prince sat down on a stone, and lifted his eyes towards the night sky.

'I wonder,' he said, 'do the stars glow so that some day everyone can find a way back to their own? Look at my planet. It is directly above us. But how far away it is!'

'It is beautiful,' said the snake. 'So what brings you here?'

'You are an odd creature,' he said at last, 'no thicker than a
finger . . .'

'I've been having some trouble with a flower,' said the little prince.

'Ah!' said the snake.

And they both fell silent.

'Where are the people?' resumed the little prince at last. 'It's a little lonely in the desert . . .'

'It is lonely when you're among people, too,' said the snake.

The little prince studied him for a long time:

'You are an odd creature,' he said at last, 'no thicker than a finger . . .'

'But more powerful than the finger of a king,' said the snake.

At this the little prince gave a smile:

'You are not so very powerful. You don't even have legs. You cannot even travel.'

'I can transport you farther than any ship,' said the snake.

He coiled himself around the little prince's ankle, like a gold bracelet.

'Whomever I touch,' the snake spoke again, 'I return them to the earth from whence they came. But you are made of purer stuff, and you come from a star.'

The little prince said nothing.

'I pity you, so frail, on this Earth of granite. I can help you, some day, should you grow too homesick for your planet. I could —'

'Oh, yes! I understand you perfectly,' said the little prince. 'But tell me, why do you always speak in riddles?'

'I solve them, one and all,' said the snake.

And they both fell silent.

XVIII

The little prince crossed the desert and met with only a solitary flower. It was a flower with three petals, a flower of no importance.

'Good day,' said the prince.

'Good day,' said the flower.

'Where are the people?' the little prince asked, politely.

The flower had once seen a desert caravan pass by.

'The people? There are some, I believe – maybe six or seven. I caught sight of them, several years back. But one never knows where to find them. The wind drives them

hither and thither. You see, they have no roots, which makes life very difficult for them.'

'Goodbye,' said the little prince.

'Goodbye,' said the flower.

XIX

The little prince climbed a high mountain. The only mountains he had ever known were the three volcanoes, which came up to his knees. And the extinct volcano used to serve him as a footstool. 'From a mountain as high as this,' he therefore said to himself, 'I'll be able to see the whole planet at a glance, and all the people.' But he could see nothing, except the peaks of some rocks, as sharp as needles.

'Good day,' he said, just in case.

'Good day . . . good day . . . good day . . .' answered the echo.

'Who are you?' said the little prince.

'Who are you . . . who are you . . . who are you . . .' replied the echo.

'Be my friends, I am all alone,' he said.

'I am all alone . . . all alone . . . all alone . . .' replied the echo.

'What a peculiar planet!' he thought to himself. 'It is all dried up, full of sharp points, and very salty. And the people have no imagination. They repeat whatever you say to them. On my planet I had a flower: she was always the first to speak.'

'This planet is all dried up, full of sharp points, and very salty.'

XX

But it so happened that, after walking for a long time through sand, and rocks, and snow, the little prince finally came upon a road. And all roads lead to people.

'Good day,' he said.

He was standing in front of a garden blooming with roses.

'Good day,' said the roses.

The little prince stared at them. They all looked just like his flower.

'Who are you?' he demanded, in astonishment.

'We are roses,' said the roses.

'Oh!' said the little prince.

And he felt extremely unhappy. His flower had told him that she was alone of her kind in the universe. And here were five thousand of them, all identical, in a single garden!

'She'd be mortified,' he said to himself, 'were she to see this. She would cough tremendously and pretend to be dying, just to avoid the ridicule. And I would have to pretend to be nursing her – otherwise she really would let herself die, to humiliate me into the bargain.'

Then he went on with his thoughts: 'I used to think myself rich, with a flower that was unique; but all I had was a common rose. That and three volcanoes, which only come up to my knees – and one of those is perhaps extinct for ever. All of which does not make me a very great prince.' And, lying down in the grass, he began to cry.

XXI

It was then that the fox appeared.

'Good day,' said the fox.

'Good day,' replied the little prince politely, looking up but unable to see anything.

'Over here,' said the voice, 'under the apple tree.'

'Who are you?' said the little prince. 'You're very pretty.'

'I'm a fox,' said the fox.

'Come and play with me,' suggested the little prince. 'I am terribly sad.'

'I can't play with you,' said the fox. 'I am not tame.'

'Oh! I beg your pardon,' said the little prince.

And, lying down in the grass, he began to cry.

Then, after a moment's thought, he added:

'What does "tame" mean?'

'You are not from these parts,' said the fox. 'What are you looking for?'

'I'm looking for people. What does "tame" mean?'

'People,' said the fox, 'they have guns, and they hunt. It's a great nuisance! They also raise chickens. That is the only interesting thing about them. Are you looking for chickens?'

'No,' said the little prince. 'I am looking for friends. What does "tame" mean?'

'Something that is frequently neglected,' said the fox. 'It means "to create ties".'

'To create ties?'

'Precisely,' said the fox. 'To me, you are still only a small boy, just like a hundred thousand other small boys. And I have no need of you. And you in turn have no need of me. To you, I'm just a fox like a hundred thousand other foxes. But if you tame me, then we shall need each other. To me, you shall be unique in the world. To you, I shall be unique in the world.'

'I'm beginning to understand,' said the little prince. 'I know a flower . . . I think she must have tamed me . . .'

'Quite possible,' said the fox. 'On this Earth one sees all manner of things.'

'Oh! But that was not on Earth,' said the little prince. The fox looked rather intrigued.

'On another planet, then?'

'Yes.'

'I see. Are there huntsmen, on this other planet?'

'No.'

'How interesting. And chickens?'

'No.'

'Nothing is perfect,' sighed the fox.

But he resumed his train of thought:

'My life is very monotonous. I run after the chickens; the men run after me. All the chickens are the same; all the men are the same. Consequently, I get a little bored. But if you tame me, my days will be as if filled with sunlight. I shall know the sound of a footstep different from all the rest. Other steps make me run to earth. Yours will call me out of my foxhole, like music. And besides, look over there! You see the fields of corn? Well, I don't eat bread. Corn is of no use to me. Corn fields remind me of nothing. Which is sad. On the other hand, you hair is the colour of gold. So think how wonderful it will be when you have tamed me. The corn, which is golden, will remind me of you. And I shall come to love the sound of the wind in the field of corn . . .'

The fox fell silent and looked steadily at the little prince for a long time.

'Please,' he said, 'tame me!'

'I should like to,' replied the little prince, 'but I don't have much time. I have friends to discover and many things to understand.'

'One only ever understands what one tames. People no longer have the time to understand anything. They buy everything ready-made from the shops. But there is no shop where friends can be bought, so people no longer have friends. If you want a friend, tame me!'

'What do I have to do?' said the little prince.

'You have to be very patient,' replied the fox. 'First, you will sit down a short distance away from me, like that, in the grass. I shall watch you out of the corner of my eye and

you will say nothing; words are the source of misunderstandings. But each day you may sit a little closer to me.'

The next day the little prince came back.

'It would have been better to come back at the same time of day,' said the fox. 'For instance, if you come at four in the afternoon, when three o'clock strikes I shall begin to feel happy. The closer our time approaches, the happier I shall feel. By four o'clock I shall already be getting agitated

'For instance, if you come at four in the afternoon, when three o'clock strikes I'll begin to feel happy.'

and worried; I shall be discovering that happiness has its price! But if you show up at any old time, I'll never know when to start dressing my heart for you . . . We all need rituals.'

'What is a ritual?' said the little prince.

'Something else that is frequently neglected,' said the fox. 'It's what makes one day different from the other days, one hour different from the other hours. There is a ritual, for example, among my huntsmen. On Thursdays they dance with the village girls. So Thursday is a wonderful day for me! I can take a stroll as far as the vineyard. If the huntsmen went dancing at any old time, the days would all be the same, and I should never have a holiday.'

So the little prince tamed the fox. And when the time for him to leave was approaching:

'Oh!' said the fox. 'I am going to cry.'

'It's your own fault,' said the little prince. 'I never wished you any harm; but you wanted me to tame you . . .'

'I know,' said the fox.

'And now you are going to cry!' said the little prince.

'I know,' said the fox.

'So you have gained nothing from it at all!'

'Yes, I have gained something,' said the fox, 'because of the colour of the corn.'

Then he added:

'Go and look at the roses again. You will understand that yours is, after all, unique in the world. Then come back and say goodbye to me; as a present I will tell you a secret.'

The little prince went off to look at the roses again.

'You are nothing like my rose,' he told them. 'As yet you are nothing at all. Nobody has tamed you, and you have tamed nobody. You are as my fox used to be. He was just a fox like a hundred thousand other foxes. But I made him my friend, and now he is unique in the world.'

And the roses felt very uncomfortable.

'You are beautiful, but you are empty,' he went on. 'One could not die for you. Of course, an ordinary passer-by would think my rose looked just like you. But in herself she matters more than all of you together, since it is she that I watered; since it is she that I placed under the glass dome; since it is she that I sheltered with the screen; since it is she whose caterpillars I killed (except the two or three we saved up to become butterflies). Since it is she that I listened to, when she complained, or boasted, or when she was simply being silent. Since it is she who is my rose.'

And he went back to the fox:

'Goodbye,' he said.

'Goodbye,' said the fox. 'Now here is my secret, very simply: you can only see things clearly with your heart. What is essential is invisible to the eye.'

'What is essential is invisible to the eye,' repeated the little prince, so as to remember.

'It is the time you have wasted on your rose that makes your rose so important.'

'It is the time I have wasted on my rose . . .' repeated the little prince, so as to remember.

'People have forgotten this truth,' said the fox. 'But you must not forget. You become responsible, for ever, for what you have tamed. You are responsible for your rose.'

'I am responsible for my rose . . .' the little prince repeated, so as to remember.

XXII

'Good day,' said the little prince.

'Good day,' said the railway pointsman.

'What do you do here?' asked the little prince.

'I sort the passengers into bundles of one thousand,' said the pointsman. 'I dispatch the trains that carry them: now to the right, now to the left.'

At which moment an express train, brightly lit and rumbling like thunder, shook the pointsman's cabin as it passed.

'They're in a great hurry,' said the little prince. 'What are they looking for?'

'Not even the engine driver can answer that,' said the pointsman.

At which there rumbled past, in the opposite direction, a second brightly lit express train.

'Are they coming back already?' asked the little prince.

'Those are not the same ones,' said the pointsman. 'It's an exchange.'

'Were they not happy where they were?'

'One is never happy where one is,' said the pointsman.

At which the thunder of a third brightly lit express train rumbled past.

'Are they chasing the first passengers?' asked the little prince.

'They are chasing nothing at all,' said the pointsman. 'They are asleep inside there, or else yawning. Only the children are flattening their noses against the window panes.'

'Only the children know what they are looking for,' said the little prince. 'They waste their time over a rag doll, and it becomes very important to them; and if it's taken away from them, they cry.'

'They're the lucky ones,' said the pointsman.

XXIII

'Good day,' said the little prince.

'Good day,' said the merchant.

The merchant was selling patent pills to quench thirst: you swallow one each week, and you no longer feel the need to drink.

'Why are you selling those things?' asked the little prince.

'They're a great time-saver,' said the merchant. 'The experts have worked it out. You can save fifty-three minutes in every week.'

'And what do I do with these fifty-three minutes?'

'You do whatever you like . . .'

'For my part,' said the little prince to himself, 'if I had fifty-three minutes to spare, I would take my time walking slowly towards the nearest fountain of water.'

XXIV

It was now the eighth day since my breakdown in the desert, and I listened to the story of the merchant while drinking the last drop of my water supply.

'Well!' I said to the little prince, 'they are all very charming, these reminiscences of yours; but I have yet to mend my aeroplane, I have nothing left to drink, and I too should be happy if I could take my time walking slowly towards the nearest fountain of water!'

'My friend the fox –' the little prince began saying.

'But my dear fellow, now is too late for foxes!'

'Why is that?'

'Because we are about to die of thirst.'

He could not follow this reasoning, and replied:

'It is good to have a friend, even if you are about to die. I for one am very happy to have had a fox for a friend.'

'He does not understand the danger,' I said to myself. 'He has never been hungry or thirsty. A little sunshine is all that he needs.'

But he looked at me and read my thoughts:

'I am thirsty, too . . . Let's look for a well.'

I shrugged wearily: it is absurd to go looking for a well,

at random, in the immensity of the desert. Nevertheless we set off.

After we had walked along in silence for several hours, darkness fell and the stars began to light up. I noticed them as if in a dream, since I was slightly feverish with thirst. The little prince's words were dancing in my head.

'So you do get thirsty?' I asked him.

But he did not reply. He merely said:

'Water may also be good for the heart.'

I did not understand this, but said nothing. I knew better by now than to question him.

He was tired. He sat down. I sat down next to him. Then, after a silence, he spoke again:

'The stars are beautiful, because of a flower that cannot be seen.'

I replied, 'Yes, that is so', and watched, without saying anything, the folds of sand beneath the moonlight.

'The desert is beautiful,' he added.

Which was true. I have always loved the desert. You sit down on a sand dune. You see nothing. You hear nothing. Yet all the time something is radiating through the silence.

'What makes the desert beautiful,' said the little prince, 'is that somewhere it is hiding a well.'

To my surprise, I suddenly understood for the first time this mysterious radiation of the sands. When I was a little boy I lived in a very old house where, according to hearsay, a treasure was buried. Of course, nobody ever discovered it, nor perhaps did they even look for it. But it cast a spell over that whole house. My home was hiding a secret in the depths of its heart.

'Yes,' I said to the little prince. 'Whether it is a house, or stars, or the desert, what makes their beauty is invisible!'

'I am pleased,' he said, 'that you agree with my fox.'

Since the little prince was now falling asleep, I lifted him in my arms, and set off walking again. I felt deeply moved. I felt that I was carrying a fragile treasure. I even felt that nothing more fragile was to be found on this Earth. In the moonlight I looked at his pale forehead, his closed eyes, his locks of hair stirring in the wind, and said to myself: 'What I see here is but a shell. What is important is invisible.'

His lips were parted in what seemed like a faint smile, and I said to myself again: 'What affects me so strongly about this sleeping prince is his loyalty to a flower, to the image of a rose, which shines inside him like the flame of a lamp, even as he sleeps . . .' And I felt him to be more fragile still. A lamp needs to be shielded with care: the merest puff of wind can blow it out.

And, walking along in this fashion, I came upon the well, at daybreak.

XXV

'People leap into express trains,' said the little prince, 'but they no longer know what they're looking for. So they get agitated and go round in circles.'

And he added:

'It's not worth the trouble.'

The well we had found was not like other wells in the Sahara. Saharan wells are simple holes bored into the sand.

He laughed, touched the rope, and set the pulley in motion.

This was like a well in a village. But there was no village here, and I thought I must be dreaming.

'This is strange,' I said to the little prince. 'Everything is ready and waiting: the pulley, the bucket, the rope . . .'

He laughed, touched the rope, and set the pulley in motion. And the pulley creaked, as an old weathervane creaks when the wind has been asleep for a long time.

'Do you hear?' said the little prince. 'We have woken up the well, and it is singing.'

I did not want him to strain himself, however:

'Let me do it,' I said. 'It's too heavy for you.'

I hoisted the bucket slowly to the edge and carefully set it down. The song of the pulley was ringing in my ears, and in the still trembling water I could see the trembling sun.

'How I long for this water,' said the little prince. 'Give me some to drink.'

And I understood what he had been looking for.

I raised the bucket to his lips. He drank, his eyes closed. This water gladdened the heart. It was something other than a mere beverage. Its sweetness was born of our march beneath the stars, of the pulley's song and the exertion of my arms. It was good for the heart, like a present. When I was a little boy, the lights of the Christmas tree, the music at midnight mass, the tenderness of the smiling faces, all these together made up the radiance of the present I received.

'Where you come from,' said the little prince, 'people grow five thousand roses in one garden – and still they do not find what they are looking for.'

'No, they do not find it,' I replied.

'Yet what they are looking for could be found in a single rose, or in a handful of water.'

'That is true,' I replied.

And he added:

'But the eyes are blind. One must look with the heart.'

I had now drunk my fill of water. I breathed deeply. The desert sand, at daybreak, is the colour of honey. I was happy, too, on account of this colour of honey. Why, then, did I also feel such sadness?

'You must keep to your promise,' said the little prince gently, after sitting down beside me again.

'What promise?'

'You know – a muzzle for the sheep. I have to be responsible for my flower!'

I took the rough sketches from my pocket. The little prince glanced over them and said, laughing:

'Your baobabs – they look more like cabbages.'

'Oh!'

And I had been so proud of my baobabs!

'Your fox's ears ... Well, they look more like horns. And they're too long!'

He laughed again.

'That is not fair, my little fellow; I have only ever been able to draw the outsides of boas and the insides of boas.'

'Oh! you'll manage,' he said. 'Children will understand.'

So I sketched him a muzzle. But my heart felt tight as I handed it to him.

'You have plans that I do not know about . . .'

He made no reply. Then he said:

'You know – the day I fell to Earth ... Tomorrow will be the anniversary.'

After a moment's silence, he went on:

'I landed very near to where we are now.'

He blushed.

Again, without knowing why, I felt a strange sorrow. One question, however, occurred to me:

'It was not by accident, then, on the morning when I met you – a week ago – that you were walking along like that, all alone, a thousand miles from human habitation? You were on your way back to the place where you landed?'

The little prince blushed again.

And I added, hesitantly:

'Because of its being the anniversary, perhaps?'

The little prince blushed once more. He never answered questions – but when somebody blushes that means 'yes', doesn't it?

'Ah!' I said to him. 'Now I am frightened.'

But he interrupted me:

'Now you must work. You must set off back to your engine. I shall wait for you here. Come back tomorrow evening.'

But I was not reassured. I remembered the fox: you run the risk of a few tears when you allow yourself to be tamed . . .

XXVI

Next to the well were the remains of an old stone wall. When I returned from my labours, the next evening, I could see from a distance my little prince sitting on top of it, his legs dangling. Then I heard his voice, saying:

'So you cannot remember? But this is not the exact spot!'

Another voice must have replied, for he answered back:

'Yes, of course! It is the right day, but this is not the place.'

I kept walking towards the wall. Still I could not see or hear anyone. However, the little prince answered again:

'But of course. You will see where my tracks begin in the sand. You have only to wait for me there. I'll be there tonight.'

I was now sixty yards from the wall, but still I could see nothing.

After a silence, the little prince spoke again:

'And your poison is good? You are sure not to make me suffer for long?'

I came to a halt. There was a lump in my throat, but still I did not understand.

'Now go away,' he said. 'I want to get down.'

At which I lowered my eyes to the base of the wall, and leaped into the air. There, rearing up before the little prince, was one of those yellow snakes that can dispatch you from this life in thirty seconds. Rummaging through my pockets for my revolver I started running. But at the noise I made the snake slid smoothly across the sand, like the last spurt of a dying fountain, and slipped unhurriedly between the stones with a light metallic sound.

I reached the wall just in time to catch the little prince in my arms; his face was as white as snow.

'What nonsense is this! So now you talk to snakes?'

I had loosened the yellow scarf he always wore round his neck. I moistened his temples and made him drink some water. And now I did not dare to question him further. He looked at me solemnly and put his arms round my neck. I

'Now go away,' he said. 'I want to get down.'

could feel his heart beating, like a dying bird brought down by rifle shot. He said:

'I am happy you found what you needed for your machine. Now you'll be able to return home.'

'How did you know that!'

I had just been coming to tell him the news that, against all odds, my efforts had succeeded.

He made no answer to my question, but he added:

'I, too, am returning home, today.'

Then, in a sad voice:

'It is a lot further away . . . a lot more difficult . . .'

I sensed clearly that something extraordinary was happening. I was holding him in my arms like a child, and yet he seemed to be sliding into an abyss, and I could do nothing to keep him back.

His gaze was solemn, lost in the far distance.

'I have your sheep. I have the box for the sheep. And I have the muzzle . . .'

He gave a melancholy smile.

I waited, for a long time. I felt him reviving little by little.

'Little fellow, you have been afraid.'

Of course he had been afraid! But he laughed softly:

'I shall be far more afraid this evening . . .'

Once again I felt myself chilled by a sense of the irreparable. And I realized I could not endure the thought of never hearing that laughter again. It was for me like a fountain in the desert.

'Little fellow, I want to hear your laughter again.'

But he said:

'Tonight, it will be a year . . . My star will be directly above the spot where I fell to Earth a year ago.'

'Little fellow, surely this story about a snake and a meeting place and a star is all a bad dream.'

But he did not answer. He said:

'What is important cannot be seen.'

'Yes, I know.'

'It's the same as with the flower. If you love a flower that lives on a star, it is sweet to look up at the night sky. All the stars are in bloom.'

'Yes, I know.'

'It's the same as with the water. What you gave me to drink was a kind of music, because of the pulley and the rope . . . Do you remember . . . how good it was?'

'Yes, I know.'

'At night, you will look up at the stars. Mine is too small to point out to you. It is better that way. For you, my star will be just one of many stars. That way, you will love watching all of them . . . They will all be your friends. What is more, I am going to give you a present.'

He laughed once more.

'Ah! little prince! How I love to hear your laugh!'

'And that is my present – just that . . . As it was when we drank the water . . .'

'What are you trying to say?'

'The stars men follow have different meanings. For some people – travellers – the stars are guides. For others they are merely little lights in the sky. For others still – the scientists – they are problems to be solved. For my businessman they meant gold. But for all these people, the stars are silent. For you, the stars will be as they are for no one else.'

'What are you·trying to say?'

'At night, when you look up at the sky, since I shall be living on a star, and since I shall be laughing on a star, for you it will be as if all the stars are laughing. You alone will have stars that can laugh!'

And he laughed again.

'And when you have got over your loss (for we always do), you'll be happy to have known me. You will always be my friend. You will want to laugh with me. And sometimes you will open your window – just like that, for the sake of opening it – and your friends will be amazed to see you laughing as you look up at the sky. Then you'll say to them: "Yes, it's the stars; they always make me laugh!" And they'll think you are crazy. I will have played a mean trick on you.'

And he laughed again.

'As if, instead of stars, I'd given you a string of little laughing bells . . .'

And he laughed again. Then he became serious once more:

'Tonight – you know . . . Do not come.'

'I won't leave you.'

'I shall seem to be very sick. I shall even seem to be dying. That is how it must be. Don't come to watch that, it is not worth the trouble.'

'I won't leave you.'

But he was anxious.

'If I tell you this, it is also because of the snake. He must not bite you. Snakes are spiteful. They can bite just for the fun of it.'

'I won't leave you.'

But something seemed to reassure him:

'I suppose it's true that they have no poison left for a second bite.'

That night I did not notice him setting off. He slipped away without a sound. When I managed to catch up with him he was walking resolutely along, with a rapid step. He merely said:

'Ah! there you are . . .'

And he took my hand. But he soon began fretting again:

'You were wrong to come. It will upset you. I shall seem to be dead and it will not be true . . .'

I said nothing.

'You understand . . . It is too far. I cannot take this body along with me. It is too heavy.'

I said nothing.

'Left behind, it will only be an old cast-off shell. There is nothing sad about an old shell.'

I said nothing.

He began to lose heart. But he made one further effort:

'It will be rather nice, you know. I too shall look up at the stars. All the stars will be wells with rusty pulleys. All the stars will pour water out for me to drink.'

I said nothing.

'It will be amusing, do you see? You will have five hundred million little bells, and I shall have five hundred million fountains of water . . .'

And now he fell silent too, for he was crying.

'Here is the spot. Let me take the next step alone.'

And he sat down, because he was afraid.

Then he added:

'You know – my flower . . . I am responsible for her! And she is so weak! She is so naive! She has four tiny little thorns to protect her against the world.'

Now I sat down too, because I could no longer stand. He said:

'Well. That is all.'

Still he hesitated a little; then he got to his feet. He took one step forward. I was motionless.

There was nothing, except a flash of yellow near his ankle. He stood stock still for an instant. He did not cry out. He fell as gently as a tree falls. There was not even any sound, because of the sand.

XXVII

And now, of course, six years have already passed . . . I have never told this story before. The friends who saw me again on my return were very happy to see me alive. I seemed sad, but I said to them: 'It's exhaustion.'

Now I have got over my loss a little. Which is to say . . . not entirely. But at least I know that he returned safely to his planet, for at daybreak I could not find his body. It was not such a heavy body . . . And at night I love listening to the stars. They are like five hundred million little bells.

Here is an extraordinary thing. When I drew the muzzle for the little prince, I forgot to add the leather strap! He will never have been able to attach the muzzle to the sheep. Then I wonder aloud to myself: 'What has happened on his planet? Perhaps the sheep has eaten the flower after all.'

Sometimes I say to myself: 'Of course not! The little prince shuts in his flower every night under her glass dome, and he keeps a close watch on his sheep.' And then I am happy. And all the stars laugh softly.

At other times I say to myself: 'Everyone's attention wanders sooner or later, and once is enough! One evening he forgot the glass dome, or else the sheep got out in the night, without any noise.' And then the little bells all turn to tears!

He fell as gently as a tree falls.

Here, then, is a great mystery. For you who love the little prince, as for me, nothing in the universe can be the same if somewhere – we do not know where – a sheep we have never met has or has not eaten a rose.

Look up at the sky. Ask yourselves: has the sheep eaten the flower or not? And you will see how everything changes . . .

And no grown-up will ever understand the significance of this!

This, to me, is the loveliest and saddest landscape in the world. It is the same landscape as on the preceding page, but I have drawn it one more time to show it to you properly. It was here that the little prince appeared on Earth, and then disappeared. Look closely at this landscape, so as to be sure to recognize it, should you travel one day to the African desert. And if you happen to pass this spot, I beg you not to hurry, but wait for a moment directly beneath the star! And if a child comes up to you, and laughs, and has golden hair, and does not answer your questions, you shall easily guess who it is. In which case, be a good boy or girl! Do not leave me in such a sorry state: write quickly and tell me that he has returned . . .

LETTER TO A HOSTAGE

I

When, in December 1940, I crossed Portugal on my way to the United States, Lisbon seemed to me a sort of paradise, bright but sad. There was much talk at the time of an impending invasion, and Portugal was clinging on to the illusion of her good fortune. Lisbon, which had set up the most enchanting of Exhibitions, was smiling a little wanly, like a mother who has no news of her son at the front, but tries to save him by an act of faith: 'My son is alive, look – I am smiling.' And so Lisbon was saying: 'Look how happy, how calm and brightly lit I am.' Yet the whole of the Continent loomed over Portugal like some threatening mountain bristling with hostile tribes. Lisbon on holiday was defying Europe: 'Who would make a target of me when I am taking such pains not to hide! When I am so vulnerable!'

Where I was coming from, the towns at night were the colour of cinders in a grate. I had become unused to light of any kind, and this gleaming capital made me vaguely uneasy. In poorly lit districts of a city, the diamonds in a bright shop-window attract suspicious characters. You can feel them prowling. So, too, I could feel the night of Europe looming over Lisbon, the air alive with roving bomber squadrons, sniffing the treasure from afar.

But Portugal preferred to ignore the appetite of this monster. She refused to credit the omens. Instead, with a desperate confidence, she talked of art. Who would dare to destroy her amid her religion of art? Portugal displayed all her wonders. Who would dare to destroy her amid her wonders? She wheeled out her great men from the past. Lacking guns or an army, she erected all her sentinels of stone – her poets, her explorers, her conquistadors – to oppose the invader's scrap iron. Lacking guns or an army, all of Portugal's past barred the road. Who would dare to destroy her amid the heritage of a glorious past?

And so, each night, I wandered with melancholy thoughts among the marvels of this Exhibition, where all was in exquisite taste, where everything bordered on perfection, even down to the delicately discreet music, chosen with such tact, flowing unobtrusively through the gardens like the simple song of a water fountain. Was this marvellous gift for proportion to disappear from the world?

And I found Lisbon, under its smile, to be a sorrier place than my blacked-out cities.

I have known, you too may have known, those slightly odd families who continue to keep a place at the table for someone who has died. They deny the irreparable. And I have never believed that this act of defiance comforts them. The dead should be treated as dead. As such, they can then regain a different kind of presence. But the families I am speaking of prevent this return. They make the dead into missing persons for eternity, into guests who will forever be late. They barter mourning for a hollow expectation. And such homes seem to me plunged into a sort of interminable wretchedness far more stifling than grief itself. For the pilot Guillaumet, the last friend I lost, Guillaumet who was shot down in the airmail service, Lord yes! for him I accept that I must go into mourning. Guillaumet will not change any further.* He will never again be present, but nor will he ever be absent. I have yielded up his place at my table, that futile snare, and turned him into what he truly is: a dead friend.

Portugal, on the other hand, was attempting to hold on to happiness, keeping its place at the table, its illuminations, its music. Everyone in Lisbon was playing at being happy, so that even God might join in the pretence.

Lisbon also owed its atmosphere of sadness to the presence of certain refugees. I do not mean those banished souls in search of a place of refuge, immigrants in quest of a land to make fruitful with their toil. I am speaking of those who expatriate themselves, far from the misery of their near ones, in order to find a safe place for their money.

Unable to find lodgings in the city itself, I was staying at Estoril, near the Casino. I had just come out of solid fighting: my air squadron, which for nine whole months flew uninterruptedly over Germany, had, in the course of a single German offensive, lost three-quarters of its crew. Returning home, I had experienced the gloomy atmosphere of slavery and the menace of starvation. I had lived through the dense night of our cities. And here, a mere step away from all of that, the Casino at Estoril was thronged nightly with pleasure-seeking ghosts. Noiseless Cadillacs, as though bound for some real destination, would deposit them on the fine sand at the porch of the Casino. They were dressed for

---

* Saint-Exupéry's colleague with the Latécoère company in North Africa and South America and his closest friend, Henri Guillaumet was killed in late 1940 by an Italian fighter pilot who mistook his transport for a British aircraft. Saint-Exupéry wrote shortly afterwards: 'I am not complaining. I have never known how to feel sorry for the dead.'

dinner, as in the past, displaying starched shirt-fronts or pearls. Each night they invited each other to these make-believe meals, where they had nothing to say to each other.

Afterwards, they would play baccarat or roulette, according to their means. Sometimes I went along to watch. I felt neither indignation nor irony, only a vague anguish. The kind one feels at the zoo, facing the survivors of some extinct species. They took their places round the tables, crowding up to some austere-looking croupier, trying to feel hope, despair, alarm, envy, jubilation. Just like the living. They staked fortunes which perhaps at that very moment had lost all meaning. They used currency which was perhaps obsolete. The shares in their strong-boxes were perhaps backed up by factories already confiscated or being flattened by bombs. Their bills were drawn on the planet Sirius. Reliving the past, they forced themselves to behave as if the world had not been falling apart for however many months, as if their excitement was real, as if their cheques were covered, as if the conventions they lived by were to last for ever. It was hallucinatory. Like a puppet ballet. But it depressed one.

Possibly, they felt nothing at all. I gave up trying to understand, and went down to the shore for some air. And the sea at Estoril, the timid sea of a seaside resort, seemed also to be part of the game. It extended a single languorous wave out into the gulf, like an outmoded dress with its train, glittering in the moonlight.

I met up with my refugees again on the steamer to New York. And the steamer, too, diffused a vague air of anguish. This boat was transferring these rootless plants from one continent to another. I thought to myself: 'I like being a traveller, but I should hate to be an emigrant. So much that I learned at home would be useless to me anywhere else.' Yet here were my emigrants taking their little address-books out of their pockets, those remnants of an identity. Still playing at being somebody, clinging with all their might to the ceremonies of meaning. 'Yes, I am so and so,' they would say, 'from such and such a town . . . A friend of X . . . Do you happen to know Y . . .?'

Then they told you the story of a friend, or the story of some responsibility, or of some moral lapse, or any story that would link them with anything whatsoever. Yet, since they were expatriating themselves, nothing from that past could be of further use to them now. It was still all warm, fresh and palpitating, as lovers' keepsakes are at first. You make a packet of the tender missives. You add a token or two. You tie it all together with great care. At first the relic emanates a melancholy charm. Then some blonde creature with blue eyes passes by, and the keepsake withers on the stalk. So, too, the childhood friend, the responsibilities, the native town, the memories of home – everything fades that no longer has a function.

They knew this, of course. Just as Lisbon played at being happy, they only pretended to believe they would soon be returning home. How sweet is the exile of the prodigal son! But that is not the real exile, since back home the family dwelling still stands. Whether someone is absent in the next room, or on the other side of the planet, there is no essential difference. The presence of a friend who is far away can sometimes feel denser than his physical presence in a room. As is the case with prayer. And never did I love home more than when I was in the Sahara. Never were betrothed couples closer than when sixteenth-century Breton sailors used to double the Horn and grow old struggling against a wall of contrary winds. From the moment they set out, their return had begun. And it was their return they were preparing, each time they hoisted the sails with massive hands. The shortest route from Breton port to the beloved's house lay round Cape Horn.

My emigrants, on the other hand, were like Breton sailors whose betrothed had been spirited away. No Breton girl would ever place her humble lamp in the window for them. These were not prodigal sons, or they were prodigal sons with no home to return to. This is when the real voyage begins, the voyage out of oneself.

How to remake oneself? How to rebuild in oneself the dense skein of memories? The ghost ship on which I travelled was, like limbo, overflowing with souls to be born. The only individuals on board who seemed real, so real one would have liked to touch them with a finger, were those who – part and parcel of the vessel, and ennobled by actual duties – carried dishes, polished brass, brushed shoes and waited with vague contempt upon the dead. It was not poverty that earned the emigrants the faint scorn of the crew. It was not money that was lacking, but density. They were no longer members of this or that family, claimed by this or that friend, by this or that responsibility. They acted the part, but it was no longer believable. No one needed them; no one wanted to make demands on them. What a miracle it is, the telegram that shatters your peace, that gets you up in the night and urges you to the station. 'Hurry! I need you.' We quickly discover in life the friends who will help us. But we only slowly deserve those who demand to be helped. No one hated these ghosts of mine, no one envied them, no one pestered them. Nor did anyone love them with the only love that matters. I thought to myself: the moment they get ashore they will be whisked off to cocktail parties to welcome them, dinners to console them. But who will bang on their doors demanding entry? 'Open up, it's me!' One must nurse a child at the breast for a long time before it learns to demand. One must cultivate friends for a long time before they demand the dues of friendship. One must have ruined oneself for generations keeping a crumbling chateau in repair before one learns to love it.

II

And so I said to myself: 'The main thing is that, somewhere, what one has lived through should be preserved intact. Customs. Family reunions. A house and its memories. The main thing is to live for the return.' And I felt menaced through and through by the tenuousness of the distant poles on which I myself depended. I was on the verge of finding myself for the first time in a real desert, and I began to understand a mystery that had puzzled me for a long time.

I lived for three years in the Sahara. Like so many others, I, too, was set dreaming by its magic. Whoever has known life in the Sahara, where everything is or seems but solitude and privation, mourns those years as the finest of their life. Phrases like 'nostalgia for the sands', 'nostalgia for solitude, for space' are merely literary formulas and explain nothing. But now, for the first time, on board this steamer packed and swarming with passengers, it seemed to me that I understood the desert.

True, as far as the eye can see, the Sahara offers only uninterrupted sand – or more precisely, the aspect of a pebbly shore, since dunes are the exception. One is eternally immersed in the very stuff of boredom. And yet, invisible divinities are weaving a network of directions, of declivities and signs, a secret and vibrant musculature. Monotony vanishes. There everything has its proper place. Even the silence is not like other silences.

There is a silence of peace, when the tribes are pacified and the evening coolness is restored; when it seems as if one has moored, sails furled, in some quiet harbour. There is a noonday silence, when the sun suspends all thought and movement. There is a false silence, when the north wind drops and the insects suddenly arrive, blown like pollen from the oases of the interior, heralding the sand storm from the East. There is a silence of conspiracy, when one knows that some distant tribe is in ferment. There is a silence of mystery, when the Arabs start up their incomprehensible palavers. There is a tense silence, when the messenger is late returning; a piercing silence, when one holds one's breath to listen; a melancholy silence, when one remembers whom one loves.

Everything becomes polarized. Each star fixes a precise direction. They are all stars of the Magi, each serving its own god. One star points the direction of a distant well, difficult to reach. And the distance separating you from that well crushes you like some rearing battlement to be scaled. Another star points the direction of a dried-up well. And the very star itself seems arid. And the distance separating you from the dried-up well is dead level. Yet another star guides you towards a secret oasis, whose praise the nomads have sung to you but which is barred by rebel tribes. And the sand separating you from this oasis seems like a fairy greensward. Another star points the direction of some white town in the South, as delectable as a fruit into which you could sink your teeth. Another star points you to the sea.

Lastly, there are the almost imaginary poles which magnetize this desert from afar: a house where one lived as a child and which remains vivid in memory; a friend of whom one knows nothing except that he is alive.

And so you feel yourself tensed and vitalized by the force field that by turns draws and repels, solicits and resists. You find yourself solidly rooted – fixed and installed at the centre of all these compass points.

Just as the desert offers no tangible rewards, just as there is nothing to see or hear, so one is forced to concede – since one's inner life, far from weakening, is fortified there – that man is animated primarily by invisible promptings. Man is governed by the spirit. In the desert I am worth as much as my gods.

So if, on board my melancholy steamer, I felt myself rich in orientations that were still intact, if I inhabited a planet that was still alive, it was thanks to certain friends lost behind me in the night of France, friends whose existence I began to feel was essential to me.

Decidedly, France to me was neither an abstract goddess nor some historian's concept, but truly a living substance on which I depended, a network of ties by which I was governed, an ensemble of poles which shaped the contours of my heart. I needed to believe that those on whom I depended for my orientations were more fixed and enduring than myself. So as to know where to return to. So as to continue existing.

In them my country dwelt in its entirety, and it lived through them in my own person. For one who navigates the seas, a continent is epitomized in the simple flash of a few beacons. A beacon gives no measure of distance. Its light flashes upon the eye, and that is all. Yet all the wonders of a continent dwell in that one star.

So today, when France, in the aftermath of total occupation, has with all its cargo passed wholly into silence – like a ship steaming without lights, no one knows whether it will survive the perils of the sea – the fate of each of those I love torments me more than some incurable illness. I find I am menaced to the core by their fragility.

The one who haunts my memory tonight is fifty years of age. He is ill. And he is a Jew. How will he survive the German terror? To imagine him as still drawing breath, I must force myself to think that he is unknown to the occupier, secretly sheltered behind the fine rampart of silence built by the peasants of his village. Only then can I believe he is still alive. Only then, strolling far into the empire of his friendship, which is without frontiers, can I think of myself not as an emigrant, but as a traveller. For the desert is not where one thinks it is. The Sahara is more alive than a metropolis, and the most teeming city is emptied of life if the essential poles of existence are demagnetized.

III

How, then, does life erect these lines of force by which we live? What is the origin of the pressure that draws me towards the house of this particular friend? What are the key moments that make his presence one of the poles I need? What secret events shape our affections, and, through these, our love of our homeland?

The real miracles make no noise. The crucial events in a life are unobtrusive. Of that moment I wish to describe, there is so little to say that I must go over it again as in a dream and describe it to the friend whom it concerns.

It was on a day before the war, on the banks of the Saône, near Tournus. We had picked a restaurant for lunch with a wooden balcony overhanging the river. Our elbows were resting on a plain wooden table, scored by knives, and we had ordered two Pernods. Your doctor forbade you spirits, but on special occasions you cheated. This was one such occasion. We could not tell why, but it was an occasion. What made us so lighthearted was less tangible even than the quality of the light. And so you decided to order the Pernod that marked special occasions. And since, a few steps away, two men were unloading a barge, we invited them to join us. We called down to them from the balcony. And they came, just like that. It seemed so obvious to invite these friends, because of the invisible sense of festivity possessing us, which was so contagious that they responded to our call. So we sat together, drinking each other's health.

It felt good to be in the sun. The poplars on the opposite

bank, the plain stretching to the horizon, were bathed in its warm honey. And we went on getting more and more cheerful without knowing why. Everything made us feel at ease: the clear sunlight, the flowing river, the food, the bargees who joined us, the maid who served us with a sort of natural grace, as though presiding over some everlasting feast. We were wholly at peace, sheltered from the disorders of civilization. We experienced a perfect state where, with every wish fulfilled, nothing remained for us to reveal to each other. We felt purified, upright, lambent, forgiving. We could not have said what truth was being thus manifested. But the dominant feeling was of a certitude verging on pride.

Through us, the universe was proving its benevolence. The nebulae had clustered, the planets had solidified, the first amoeba had formed, and life's vast labour had led from amoeba to man – so that all would converge harmoniously, through us, in the pleasure of this moment! It was not so bad, as achievements go.

And so we relished this mute communion and these quasi-religious rites. Lulled by the movements of the sacerdotal maidservant, the four of us drank together like the worshippers of one religion, though none of us could have said which. One of the bargees was Dutch, the other German. The latter had some time ago fled the Nazis, who were pursuing him for being a Communist, or a Trotskyist, or a Catholic, or a Jew (I forget the precise label under which he was outlawed). But at this moment in time the bargee bore no resemblance to any label. It was what was inside that counted. The human leaven. He was, quite simply, a friend. And we were in harmony, all of us, as between friends. You and I, the bargees, the maidservant.

But in harmony as to what, exactly? The Pernod? The meaning of life? The mellow sunlight? That, too, we could not have explained. But this harmony was so complete, and its substance, though impossible to put a name to, was so solidly rooted in a faith, that we would willingly have barricaded this rustic inn, endured a siege and died at our posts to preserve it.

What substance? . . . This, of course, is where it is difficult to say what I mean. I risk capturing the reflection, not the essence. The truth leaks away between the inadequate words. It would be obscurantist to suggest we would have fought merely to preserve some nuance in the bargees' smile, in your smile and mine, in the maid's smile, some miracle in the sunlight, which had taken such pains, over so many millions of years, to achieve – through us – this moment.

The essential, as usual, is imponderable. The essential here, so it seems, was but a smile. But often the essential is indeed a smile. One is paid by a smile, repaid by a smile, quickened by a smile. And there is a kind of smile, too, that is a death warrant. However, since it was a smile that freed us so completely from the anguish of these times, vouch-safing certitude, hope and peace, today, in order to express myself better, I shall tell you the story of another smile.

IV

It was when I was reporting on the Civil War in Spain. I had been indiscreet enough, one morning at three a.m., to watch undercover some material being secretly loaded at a goods yard. The bustle of the work gangs and the darkness seemed to favour my indiscretion. But a few of the anarchist militiamen took notice of me.

It all happened very quietly. Before I had any idea of their elastic and silent approach, they had already closed gently around me, like fingers. A gun barrel was pressed lightly to my stomach, in an ominous silence. I had no choice but to raise my arms.

I noticed that they gazed not at my face, but at my tie (anarchist fashions did not encourage such aesthetic appendages). My muscles tensed. I waited for the volley of shots, since this was a time when prompt judgements were the order of the day. But there were no shots. After a few moments of utter suspension, during which the work gangs seemed to be performing a dream ballet in some remote world, my anarchists, with an imperceptible nod, signalled for me to walk on ahead, and we set off in no particular hurry across the sidings. My capture had taken place in total silence, without so much as a wasted gesture. Life in the ocean depths must be like this.

Soon I entered a basement converted into a guardroom. In the dim light of a cheap oil lamp other militiamen were dozing, their rifles between their knees. Some words were exchanged, in expressionless tones, with the patrol which had brought me in. Somebody searched me.

I can speak Spanish, but not Catalan. I understood, however, that they were asking for my papers. I had forgotten them at the hotel. I said: 'Hotel . . . Journalist . . .' without knowing whether the words meant anything. The militiamen passed my camera from hand to hand as though it were proof of my guilt. Some of the yawning figures, slumped in their rickety chairs, got to their feet out of boredom and leaned against the wall.

For my main impression was of boredom. Boredom and sleep. These men's capacity for paying attention had, it seemed, been worn threadbare. I would almost have preferred some sign of hostility, as a token of human contact. But they would not honour me with any sign of anger, or even of reprobation. I tried several times to protest in Spanish. My protests fell on deaf ears. They observed me, impassively, as they would have watched a goldfish in a bowl.

They were waiting. Waiting for what? For one of their number to return? For dawn to break? I said to myself: 'They are perhaps waiting to feel hungry . . .'

And then I thought: 'They'll do something stupid. This is completely ridiculous! . . .' What I felt – far more than anxiety – was disgust at the absurdity of it all. I said to myself: 'If they unfreeze, if they feel like doing anything at all, they'll shoot me.'

Was I in real danger? Who knows? Were they still ignorant of the fact that I was not a saboteur, or a spy, but a journalist? That my identity papers really were at the hotel? Had they made a decision? To do what?

I knew little about these men, except that they shot people without much soul-searching. Revolutionary vanguards, of whatever party, do not hunt men (the individual does not interest them) but symptoms. Adverse truth, to them, is like an epidemic. The first sign of a dubious symptom, and the bearer is rushed to the isolation ward. To the cemetery. That was why this cross-examination, which from time to time fell on my hearing in vague monosyllables, and of which I understood nothing, seemed so sinister. A roulette was playing with my life. This was also why I felt the strange urge to impress my existence upon them, to shout out something about myself that would convince them of my reality. My age, for instance! A man's age is something that creates an impression. It is the epitome of his whole life. It has accrued slowly, the maturity that is his alone. It has come together in the teeth of all the obstacles conquered, the grave illnesses overcome, the pains that flesh is heir to, the despairs surmounted and the risks courted, of most of which he knew nothing at the time.

It has come about by way of so many desires, hopes, regrets, forgettings, love. What a cargo of experience, of memories, a man's age represents! In spite of the pitfalls, jolts, ruts, he has managed to keep going, bumps and all, like a solidly built wagon. And now, thanks to the obstinate convergence of fortune, he has made it to thirty-seven years of age. And the wagon, if it please God, will bear its load of memories yet further. And so I said to myself: 'This is where I've come to. I am thirty-seven.' I would have liked to burden my judges with this confession . . . But they were no longer questioning me.

It was then that the miracle happened. Oh, a modest enough miracle. I had no cigarettes, and since one of my gaolers was smoking, I gestured to him, with a vague smile, to let me have one. First the man stretched his limbs, then he slowly passed his hand over his brow, raised his eyes towards me (no longer at my tie but at my face) and, to my stupefaction, smiled faintly back. It was like the break of day.

The miracle did not untangle the plot so far: it simply wiped it out, as light banishes dark. No drama had taken place. Nothing in the visible world was altered by this miracle. The cheap oil lamp, the paper-strewn table, the men leaning against the wall, the colour of things, their smell – everything remained as it was. But everything was transformed in its essence. That smile released me. It was a sign, as final, as clear in its immediate consequences, as irreversible as the appearance of the sun. It opened a new era. Nothing had changed, everything had changed. The paper-strewn table came to life. The oil lamp came to life. The walls came to life. The boredom secreted by the dead things in this cellar was dissipated as though by enchantment. As though an invisible blood supply had begun to circulate again, reconnecting all things as part of the same body, and restoring significance to them.

The men had not moved; but whereas a moment ago they had seemed more remote than some prehistoric species, now they emerged into an existence continuous with mine. I felt an extraordinary sensation of presence. Exactly that: presence! And I experienced my kinship with them.

The youth who smiled, and who, a moment earlier, had been but a task, a tool, a sort of monstrous insect, now revealed himself to be a little awkward, even timid. Not that this terrorist was any less brutal than the next one, but the advent of the man in him so illumined all that was vulnerable. We men put on great airs, but in our hearts there is hesitancy, doubt, all the fret that we feel.

Still nothing had been said. Yet everything was resolved. I put my hand, in gratitude, on the militiaman's shoulder when he handed me the cigarette. And then, the ice broken, the others too turned into men again, and I entered into their general smile as if entering a new and free country.

I entered into their smile, as, in the past, I had entered the smiles of our rescuers in the Sahara. The friends who found us after days of searching, having landed as close as they dared, came striding towards us, swinging the water skins as visibly as they could. The smile of the rescuers, when I was a castaway; the smile of the castaways, when I was a rescuer – I remember this as a homeland in which I found all happiness. True pleasure is the pleasure of sharing. Being rescued was but its occasion. And water could not bind spells were it not, in the first place, the gift of man's goodwill.

The care of the sick, the welcome proffered to the exile, the act of forgiveness itself, these have meaning on account of the smile that illuminates the occasion. We come together in the smile that is beyond language, caste or political party. We are all, I and mine, worshippers of one religion, it and its rites.

V

Is not this capacity for joy the most precious fruit of the civilization that is ours? A totalitarian tyranny, too, might satisfy us in our material needs. Except that we are not beasts to be fattened. Prosperity and creature comforts alone could never fulfil all our needs. For those of us brought up to believe in human respect, the simplest encounters often bear the heaviest meaning.

Human respect! There is the touchstone. For as long as the Nazi respects only what resembles him, he respects nothing but himself. In rejecting contradiction he destroys all hope of man's ascent, establishing for a thousand years in its place the robotism of the ant-heap. Order for order's sake castrates man of his essential power, which is to transform both the world and himself. Life creates order, but order does not create life.

It seems to me that our ascent is far from complete, that tomorrow's truth grows out of yesterday's error, and that the contradictions to be overcome are the very compost of growth. We recognize as ours even those who differ from us. But what a strange kinship! One that is based on the future, not on the past. On the end, not on the origins. We are each other's pilgrims, who toil along different roads towards the same meeting place.

But today human respect, the very condition of our ascent, is threatened. The creakings of the modern world have led us into darkness. The problems themselves have no coherence; the solutions contradict each other. Yesterday's truth is dead, tomorrow's still to be constructed. No valid synthesis can be glimpsed, and each of us holds but a fragment of the truth. Lacking the proofs that would make them unassailable, the political religions resort to violence. And so, divided as to the means, we risk forgetting that we are all pursuing the same end.

If the traveller following his star across the mountain becomes too absorbed in pondering ways of reaching the top, he risks forgetting which star it is that guides him. If we act merely for the sake of action, we will get nowhere. The pew attendant in the cathedral, over-zealous about the arrangement of her chairs, risks forgetting that she serves a god. So, by absorbing myself in the passion of party politics, I risk forgetting that politics are meaningless unless they serve a spiritual truth. In rare moments it is given to us to taste a certain quality in human relations: that is where our truth lies.

However urgent the call to action, it is sterile if we forget the vocation that must properly motivate it. We wish to establish human respect. Why hate each other, who are of the same camp? None of us holds the monopoly on pure intentions. I may dispute, in favour of my chosen road, the road that someone else has taken. I may criticize the workings of his logic – human reason is uncertain. But I must respect the man, the spiritual being, if he toils towards the same star.

If such respect is founded in men's hearts, mankind will certainly end by establishing the social, political, economic system that enshrines this respect. A civilization establishes itself first of all in matter, as the blind desire for a certain warmth. Thereafter, from one error to the next, we discover the road that leads to fire.

VI

This is no doubt why, my friend, I have such need of your friendship. I thirst for a companion who, standing above the litigations of reason, respects in me the pilgrim of that fire. I need occasionally to savour in advance the promised warmth, and to repose – outside myself a little – in the meeting place that is yet to be ours.

I am weary of controversy, opinionation, fanaticism. I can walk into your house without donning a uniform, without having to recite some gospel, without renouncing any part of my inner homeland. With you, I do not have to exonerate myself, to plead, to prove: I find peace, as on that afternoon at Tournus. Beyond the clumsy words, beyond the specious arguments, what you see in me is simply a man. You honour me as the ambassador of a faith, customs, particular affections. If I differ from you, far from wronging you, I add something to you. And you cross-question me as one does a returning traveller.

Feeling a need to be recognized, like all of us, I go to you for purification. It was not my turns of phrase or my actions that showed you who I am. It was the acceptance of who I am that made you indulge, when necessary, those actions and those turns of phrase. I am grateful to you for taking me as you find me. What do I want with a friend who judges me? When I welcome someone to my house, if he has a limp I ask him to sit down, not to dance.

So, my friend, I need you as a I need a high place where I can breathe freely. I need to sit beside you, once more, on the banks of the Saône, at some ramshackle little inn where we can invite two bargees to join us in celebrating a smile as calm as the day itself.

If I am still to fight in this war, I shall fight a little for you. I need you so as to keep faith with the future of that smile. I need to keep you alive. I picture you, weak, menaced, dragging your fifty years for hours on end outside some wretched grocer's, shivering under the dubious protection of a threadbare coat, merely to go on living a day or two longer. You who are so French, I feel you doubly exposed, as a Frenchman and as a Jew. How I prize a community that refuses to serve contention. We all derive from France, as from a branching tree, and I will serve your truth as you would have served mine.

For us, Frenchmen outside, what is at issue in this war is how to release the seed stock frozen by the snows of the German presence. How to succour those who have remained. How to free you in the land where your fundamental right is to spread your roots. You are forty million hostages. It is in the caves of oppression that the new truths are prepared: forty million hostages are pondering their new truth. The rest of us submit in advance to that truth.

For it is from you that we shall learn. It is not for us to bring the spiritual flame to those who nourish it already with their very being, as though with wax. Perhaps you will scarcely look at the books we write. Perhaps you will scarcely listen to the talks we give. You may well vomit back our ideas. It is not we who are rebuilding France. We can only serve her. We shall have no right, whatever we may do, to any gratitude. There is no common denominator between the task of soldier and that of hostage. It is you who are the saints.

PENGUIN MODERN CLASSICS

SOUTHERN MAIL/ NIGHT FLIGHT

ANTOINE DE SAINT-EXUPÉRY

'Some of the finest prose written this century, lyrical, at times visionary, polished and still fresh' *Spectator*

Antoine de Saint-Exupéry, an intrepid and eccentric adventurer, transferred his passion for flying to the written word by writing several classics of aviation literature, including *Southern Mail* and *Night Flight*. Based on Saint-Exupéry's trail-blazing flights for the French airmail service over the Sahara and, later, the Andes, these two novels evoke the tragic courage and nobility of the airborne pioneers who took enormous risk, flying in open cock-pits in planes that were often fragile and unstable.

'Saint-Exupéry evokes a sublime world, far from the dismal cares of earth, where man might find his true self in the reverie of flight' *Daily Telegraph*

Translated by Curtis Cate

With a Preface to *Night Flight* by André Gide

PENGUIN MODERN CLASSICS

WIND, SAND AND STARS
ANTOINE DE SAINT-EXUPÉRY

'A Conrad of the air ... Like Conrad, Saint-Exupéry is a poet of action'
André Maurois

In 1926 Antoine de Saint-Exupéry (author of the classic *The Little Prince*) began flying for the pioneering airline Latécoère – later known as Aéropostale – opening up the first mail routes across the Sahara and the Andes. *Wind, Sand and Stars* (1939) is drawn from this experience.

Interweaving stories of encounters with the nomadic Arabs and other adventures into a rich autobiographical narrative, it has its climax in the extraordinary story of Saint-Exupéry's crash in the Libyan Desert in 1936, and his miraculous survival.

Translated with an Introduction by William Rees

Penguin Modern Classics

THE OUTSIDER
ALBERT CAMUS

'The story of a beach murder, one of the century's classic novels. Blood and sand'
J. G. Ballard, *Daily Telegraph*

In his classic existential novel Camus explores the predicament of the individual
who is prepared to face the indifference of the universe courageously and alone.

Meursault leads an apparently unremarkable bachelor life in Algiers until he commits
an act of violence. His response to the incident challenges the fundamental values
of his society, a set of rules so binding that any person breaking them is considered
an alien. For Meursault it is an insult to his reason and a betrayal of his hopes; for
Camus it is the absurdity of life.

Translated by Joseph Laredo

WINNER OF THE NOBEL PRIZE FOR LITERATURE

PENGUIN MODERN CLASSICS

NAUSEA
JEAN-PAUL SARTRE

'One of the very few successful members of the genre "philosophical novel" … a young man's tour de force' Iris Murdoch

Nausea is both the story of the troubled life of the young writer, Antoine Roquentin, and an exposition of one of the most influential and significant philosophical attitudes of modern times – existentialism. The book chronicles his struggles with the realization that he is an entirely free agent in a world devoid of meaning; a world in which he must find his own purpose and then take total responsibility for his choices. A seminal work of contemporary literary philosophy, *Nausea* evokes and examines the dizzying angst that can come from simply trying to live.

Translated by Robert Baldick
With an Introduction by James Wood